FRANKLAND

A NOVEL

JAMES WHORTON, JR.

FREE PRESS

NEW YORK   LONDON   TORONTO   SYDNEY

FREE PRESS
A Division of Simon & Schuster, Inc.
1230 Avenue of the Americas
New York, NY 10020

FREE PRESS and colophon are trademarks
of Simon & Schuster, Inc.

For information about special discounts for bulk purchases,
please contact Simon & Schuster Special Sales at
1-800-456-6798 or business@simonandschuster.com

DESIGNED BY LAUREN SIMONETTI

Manufactured in the United States of America

1   3   5   7   9   10   8   6   4   2

Library of Congress Cataloging-in-Publication Data
Whorton. James, 1967–
Frankland : a novel / James Whorton, Jr.
p. cm.
I. Title.

PS3623.H6F73 2005
813'.6—dc22   2004057672

ISBN 0-7432-4448-6

To my mother and father

1

I WALKED TWENTY-TWO blocks to find a can of Fix-A-Flat in Brooklyn. Anywhere else in North America, the stuff is kept several cans deep on the store shelves, but not in New York City. At last, in a narrow-aisled bodega, I found a single can, hidden behind a basket of paraffin-coated yucca roots. There were three red price stickers on the cap, stacked carefully so that only the top price could be seen.

I got "on line" behind a white-haired woman in a black tunic. There was Latin music playing from a radio. The woman bent over at the counter, scratching at something, then straightened and began to scream in short bursts, like this: "Aah! Aah! Aah! Aah! Aah!"

The man at the register took a step back and lifted a golf club over his shoulder. "What is she screaming for?"

"I've just won ten thousand dollars!" the woman said. She moved her body to one side, and I saw she had a New

York Lottery scratch-off card pinned to the counter with both thumbs.

"You did what? Let me see," the man said. He lowered his club, and she turned the card around so he could read it right-side up. "No, no. You won a hundred. There's a decimal in there."

"A hundred? You're nuts," she said. "Get your glasses on."

He carefully slid on a pair of reading glasses, then bent over and peered at the card again. "Holy mother! You did win ten thousand! *Aaaaahhh!*"

"I told you! *Aaah! Aaah! Aaaaaaahhh!*"

New Yorkers are an excitable breed, but they're quick to settle down again. After a small crowd had gathered and dispersed, things went back to the New York version of normal. The woman tucked the winning card into her wallet and asked the man for a carton of Marlboro Lights and a bottle of Poland water. A man who'd been trying to sell some key rings on the sidewalk asked her to buy him a carton, too. She said she would buy him one pack, and a sandwich if he was hungry.

"I'm not hungry," he said.

She bought him a pack of Winstons and left. I paid for my Fix-A-Flat.

After six disappointing months in the city, this simple can of leak-sealing, tire-inflating foam was my ticket out. I walked the twenty-two blocks to where my yellow Plymouth Duster sat listing at the curb. By the time I got there, I had shaken the can quite thoroughly per the instructions. I attached the tube to the left rear tire valve and released the foam, and the tire inflated. I got on my way.

I was twenty-eight years old. The historian Arthur M. Schlesinger, Jr. had won a Pulitzer by this age. The thought depressed me, and I reminded myself that Professor Schlesinger had the benefit of some early advantages that I lacked, in addition to his no doubt considerable native intelligence. We all have to do what we can with the tools we are given. By this same age of twenty-eight, Andrew Johnson had advanced himself from tailor's apprentice to elected representative in the Tennessee General Assembly. Unlike Schlesinger, the future seventeenth president had no Exeter or Harvard behind him. He'd been taught to write by his teenage bride.

I left the city with my windows down, crossing the Verrazano Narrows Bridge, then Staten Island. The Duster could not maintain highway speed with its air conditioner running. I followed U.S. 1 through New Jersey and Pennsylvania, then into Maryland. In Baltimore I spotted a medium-sized fowl bird with an eighteen-inch tail sprinting frantically along the gutter of Belair Road. Traffic was heavy, and the bird, whose head was green with scarlet patches, was badly out of place. I later confirmed it to have been a male ring-necked pheasant.

Farther south, in the District of Columbia, I spent an hour outside the Smithsonian Institution's Arts and Industries Building eating two peanut butter sandwiches and trying to make myself feel, with all its fullness, this brief moment of my presence in the nation's capital. History is a difficult thing to imagine. Is it a line in which our lives form a tiny segment? Or is it a massive live beast to whose hump we cling? Andrew Johnson, I recalled, had in early days proposed converting the Smithsonian into a national trade school offering courses of study in carpentry, dentistry, and plumbing. What kind of man had thoughts like that?

Already the sights and strains of travel had fatigued me some. I'd gotten a later start than I'd meant to, due to some confusion with my landlady Mrs. Chouri over the security deposit. The sum was not an enormous one, but I had counted on it, especially in the light of certain inconveniences that I had quietly put up with during my six months' tenancy in her building. For example, the shower in my apartment had no shower head. There was only a threaded neck protruding from a hole chipped out between tiles. Warm, cloudy water gurgled from it. My neighbor crushed ice at all hours, on the counter top with a spoon if my ears do not lie. I hadn't complained. Then, that morning, as we walked through the apartment, Mrs. Chouri announced that my book crates had ruined her carpeting.

"They have only made a very faint imprint," I said.

"Oh no! They have seriously gouged the carpet, which affects the value of my building."

The facial absurdity of this proposition did not embarrass her. She clicked her mouth at me, bringing it closer and closer to my face, flicking her fingers at the same time in a characteristic way that she had. When she got so close that her breath moved my hair, I had to leave, deposit or not.

Can a person so easily whipped as this look forward to any success in life? I turned the question around in my mind as I sat by myself on the National Mall. I had a postcard on my knee and was attempting to pen a note to my mother, but I could not think what to say in so few words. Across the pavement, a man emerged from the Arts and Industries Building with a puffy Uncle Sam hat on his head. He stopped for a moment, perusing a brochure. The giant hat was made of satin, and it flopped to one side. The man slid the brochure into a trash barrel and wandered away.

There are two kinds of historians: those who ascribe agency to vast impersonal forces, and those who give the credit and blame to individual humans. I hold the latter view, though I sometimes have to remind myself of it. I did this now. For a change, I had a plan, and I also had an advantage. Many had studied the scandal-torn presidency of Andrew Johnson; some had the backing of universities and endowed foundations, but I had a secret lead all the others had overlooked. The lead concerned a set of Johnson papers that had been deliberately mislaid, and had stayed lost for over a century. I had reason to think I could find them. All I had to do was stay on task with an animal tenacity. Setbacks and reversals would come, but I would deal with them, drawing on my life's experience and my bit of self-knowledge as needed.

Step one had been leaving New York, the city where I developed a tic of excessive blinking. If for no other reason, I had to go away to rest my eyelids.

Step two was Tennessee. I got back on the road.

The Duster had been mine for one day. I had bought it from Mrs. Chouri's nephew. When I stepped on the gas, a blue haze filled the rearview mirror. I had noted the smoky discharge on first inspecting the car, and when I mentioned it to Mrs. Chouri's nephew he said, "What do you expect for under two thousand dollars?" This throwing the comment back in your face is the New Yorker's idiom. He assured me some smoking was normal for a car with ninety thousand miles on it. But the smoking got worse, and now, on the interstate south of Washington, the yellow Duster started to hesitate. Women and girls scowled down at me from the passenger windows of tall SUVs. The Duster slowed to about fifty miles per hour, and I switched on the hazard lights.

The miles and hours passed slowly, until just below Wytheville, Virginia, the right rear tire blew out. I steered the crippled vehicle to the side of the road and got out to look. The sun was behind some hills, and a cantaloupe-colored light washed over the roadside grass and gravel. I found a ragged hole in the side of the tire.

I opened the trunk. The jack and spare were under all of my clothes, plus the entire University of Tennessee edition of the papers of Andrew Johnson, seventeen volumes counting the supplement. I had left the carpet-ruining crates in New York, having learned in the course of many moves that to pack a car truly full, the books must go in loose.

I decided to wait for morning. I read until dark, then tried to sleep, which was difficult in the little crowded vehicle under the stars at the edge of the freeway with eighteen-wheelers hurtling past all night at an irregular frequency, shedding enormous violent air wakes that made the Duster shudder in place, and some of them blowing their loud horns. At length I dropped off into a fragmentary slumber and dreamed I was a passenger on one of those haunted-house carnival rides where arms and squeals and hatchets pop out from the darkness, and you are strapped into your seat and can hear the wheels rattling underneath you on the tracks.

Then, in my dream, I was with my father at the Hall of the Presidents at Disney World in Orlando, Florida. I was ten. A very rich and keen expectancy lay upon us as the auditorium lights dimmed and the curtain rose on a life-sized tableau of the thirty-nine American presidents. My father pointed out the current one, Ronald Reagan, towards the front in a brown suit, alongside Abraham Lincoln and the seated General Washington. I searched the back rows for the two fat presidents, Grover Cleveland and William Howard Taft, and the sideburn-wearing Chester Arthur, and the hollow-cheeked John Tyler. I knew all of their faces well, having studied them daily at school. Their printed portraits were taped up in a row above the chalkboard in our classroom. My father clutched at my arm, and the shiny-haired Reagan spoke:

"I welcome you to the Hall of the Presidents, where the chief executives of our nation have gathered to share with you the story of our America."

The president's head turned smoothly a few degrees and stopped. His spotlight faded as another one rose on Teddy Roosevelt, who had a look on his face like he was being pinched by devils. His jaw chopped open and shut when he talked. The dozen or so major presidents spoke in turn, each pivoting his head in some way or lifting an arm to emphasize a point. Woodrow Wilson was eulogizing the League of Nations when my father and I noticed a low, monotonous sound. It seemed at first like something mechanical—a noisy blower in the ventilation system, possibly—but then a rhythm of muffled speech emerged. Wilson stopped in mid-sentence, his head twisting quizzically.

"Deem me not vain or arrogant," the muffled voice said; *"yet I should be less than man if under such circumstances I were not proud of being an American citizen, for today one who claims no high descent, one who comes from the ranks of the people, stands, by the choice of a free constituency, in the second place in the government."*

"What in the hell is that noise?" Teddy Roosevelt said.

"There may be those to whom such things are not pleasing, but those who have labored for the consummation of a free Government will appreciate and cherish institutions which exclude none however obscure his origin from places of trust and distinction," the voice went on.

"It's Johnson," Woodrow Wilson said.

"It ain't me," Lyndon Baines Johnson replied.

"No. It's *Andrew* Johnson," Wilson said. "He's giving his vice presidential inauguration speech again."

"Speak not over your interlocutor, nor weary him with tedious iterations," General Washington said from his chair down in front.

"You, Senators, you who constitute the bench of the

Supreme Court of the United States, are but the creatures of the American people; your exaltation is from them; the power of this Government consists in its nearness and approximation to the great mass of the people. You, Mr. Secretary Seward, Mr. Secretary Stanton, the Secretary of the Navy. . . ."

"I cannot make out the man's words!" Franklin Delano Roosevelt exclaimed shrilly. He and Washington were the only seated presidents. "His speech is slurred!"

"The man has been drinking," Lyndon Johnson said. "He's shit-faced!"

"His jaw has no hinge," Thomas Jefferson explained.

Jefferson was correct. A spotlight found Andrew Johnson's place high on the back row of presidents and lit up his powdery white face and the obdurate blue eyes. Unlike the major presidents' mannequins, his had limbs and a head that were nonmotorized. His jaw was immobile, and he spoke through what appeared to be a narrow slit between his pale wax lips. *"Humble as I am, plebeian as I may be deemed, permit me in the presence of this brilliant assemblage to enunciate the truth that courts and cabinets, the President and his advisors, derive their power and their greatness from the people. Such an assertion of the great principles of this Government may be considered out of place, and I will not consume the time of these intelligent and enlightened persons much longer; but I could not be insensible to these great truths when I, a plebeian, elected by the people the Vice President of these United States, am here to enter upon the discharge of my duties."*

"Can it," Lyndon Johnson said.

"How'd he get drunk when his jaw won't hinge?" Harry Truman said.

"I welcome you to the Hall of the Presidents," Ronald Reagan said.

Andrew Johnson went on, unfazed. *"I, though a plebeian boy, am authorized by the principles of the Government under which I live to feel proudly conscious that I am a man, and grave dignitaries are but men."*

But then abruptly he stopped speaking, and his short, rigid frame fell forwards into the aisle with a soft crash. He was quiet.

"Thank you, Christ," Lyndon Johnson said.

"Andy has learned his lesson," Lincoln added.

My father, who was still squeezing my arm, said, "That was not at all what I expected, son."

I woke up to find the Duster's windows fogged and myself encased in a clammy sweat.

2

MANY LONG HOURS LATER, morning came, and I watched the sky turn pink through a spattered windshield. I emptied the trunk and changed the tire. The morning air was cloudy, and the ground was damp. The tire that had blown would not fit in the space where the spare had been, which meant that when I got every-thing reloaded, the trunk lid wouldn't shut. There was nothing to tie it down with but a necktie, and I was not willing to do that, so I left the trunk open. I wiped my hands on the grass and dry-brushed my teeth, and I got back onto the road.

The Duster ran poorly and there was a new note in the sound of it, a throatiness. I thought I smelled gaso-line. Around me were the shadowy, low foothills of the Appalachians, and as the mist burned off I saw sloping green pastures with cows and sheds on them, water tanks, and dark green cedar trees left to grow along fence lines. About nine o'clock ante meridiem I crossed the line into Tennessee. A building in the shape of a guitar stood between the freeway and the frontage road. It was some sort of tourist attraction but did not look open for business, and I would not have stopped if it had been. My destination was Greeneville, the city where a youthful Andrew Johnson first arrived in 1826, a runaway apprentice leading a one-eyed mule and accompanied by his brother, their mother, and her second husband.

I skipped the exits for Bristol and then Johnson City (named, incidentally, for a Johnson who was not related to the former president) and left the freeway on a narrow state route that took me some miles among small farms and wood lots, over creeks and past stone spring houses and barns. It was a winding two-lane. The question developed in my mind whether the road I was on was the one I had marked on the map. It was definitely Tennessee, though—and how satisfying it was to be here at last, after so much reading and planning. The sky was a candylike blue, the turf a nitrogen-charged green. Every curve in the road opened onto some small surprise: a picturesque farmhouse with clotheslines and tomato cages, or a tin-roofed Methodist church.

I came to a town. A service station, a grocery, and a large gray wood-frame feed mill with a Purina sign faced each other at the crossroads. Past the grocery was a brown-brick building with a fire truck in front, and next door to this was a cinder-block structure with a sign on its roof saying "MAISY RESTAURANT" in red capitals. There were a few houses set close together and also a tiny U.S. Post Office building with four white columns and a pediment bearing the legend "Pantherville, Tennessee 37612."

I was fairly certain I had made a wrong turn. My map, photocopied from an atlas in the New York City Public Library, Fifth Avenue and Forty-second Street branch, did not indicate any "Pantherville," and I had seen no signs for Greeneville. There was a slow tractor in the road, hauling a large round hay bale, and after following it patiently through town and then for the better part of a mile beyond, I hit my turn signal and accelerated past it on a straight stretch. The operator was a weather-beaten man in blue overalls and a red cap.

I was pulling back into the right lane when I saw that the Duster's temperature light had come on. At first I didn't stop; I thought a slight overheating might be something I could drive on through. But I smelled a burning odor. I cut the engine and coasted to the edge of the road with no building or pay phone in sight. Loud and slow, the tractor I had passed came out of a curve and passed me by. The operator gave me a frown and a wave.

I got out and raised the hood. I knew it would be no use, but not to look under the hood, at least, would have seemed girlish. I noted some hissing and saw that a greenish brown liquid dripped from several places, including the underside of the hood. I transferred a few volumes of the *Papers of Johnson* to the front seat— enough to allow me to close the trunk—and then I started the hike back towards Pantherville.

I make it a point to try and profit from whatever situation I find myself in. The effort itself may be morally helpful, and even if it isn't, it is an example of the most benign sort of obsessional behavior. I walked briskly, using a loping gait that was intended to loosen any potential blood clots that might have begun to accrete in my leg arteries over the previous twenty-something hours that I had spent confined in the Duster, and I observed the old fence posts that lined the bank along the road. They looked very solid, and I made up my mind to find out what variety of wood such posts were made from. The fact might serve as a choice detail in some future written passage about the region.

There were cows across the fence, standing in mud at the margin of a pond. They watched me go. The grass on their side of the fence was cropped; on my side, along the road, it was tall, and nestled in it was the type of waste one would spot along most any roadside in America: brown bottles, sodden magazines, odd bits of automobile trim, and the like. Here at the edge of the pavement was a disposable tooth-flossing tool, built like a coping saw, which some fastidious litterbug had flicked out of his window.

A vague thought came to me, and I stopped for a second. It wasn't a thought so much as a feeling—a surge of dread, to be exact. It was beginning to dawn on me that buying the Duster from Mrs. Chouri's nephew had been not only a bad move but a characteristic one. It fit right in with the series of choices I had made over the six previous months, in the course of which I had abandoned a life of secure and pleasant routine for a gamble that was almost certain to turn out badly and to teach me things about myself that I did not want to learn. What a sorry set of mistakes I had made, and was certain to continue making. Well, I knew I must put such thoughts out of my head, but the question was how to do so. Just about this time I felt something stirring near my leg. I looked down to discover that I had surprised a little gray garter snake in the grass. Frightened, it had slipped into the cuff of my trouser leg.

I have no special fear of snakes, but I just was not prepared for this one, and I began to kick my leg out very spastically many times. Improbable as it may seem, the small snake had found a cranny that fit it in my trouser cuff, and though I shook my leg violently it did not come out. I could feel its tugging weight with every kick.

A white vehicle approached in the road, rather fast. Still kicking, I moved off the pavement so as not to get hit. The ground was uneven at the edge of the road and I reached out to steady myself by touching a piece of fence wire. I received a powerful shock that sent me careening off-balance back into the road, right into the path of the oncoming vehicle, a Jeep Wagoneer with a white light flashing from its roof. I went down. The Wagoneer stopped. On my back in the road, I thrust my leg into the air and the garter snake dropped out of my cuff and onto the front of my shirt. I flipped myself along the pavement like a trout on land, and then I jumped to my feet and looked all around me for the snake, at the same time touching my clothes all over. I decided the snake had gotten away. Rather crazily I even patted my hair to make sure it was snake-free.

I went to the driver's-side window of the Wagoneer to ask for a lift into town. To my surprise the driver's seat was empty. The driver was on the passenger side, staring at me with large dark eyes.

"I need a ride into town," I said. "My car died."

She said nothing but only stared. Her mouth hung open and I saw the white tips of her teeth.

"I had a snake in my trouser cuff, if you're wondering what that business was about in the road. Then I got shocked by that fence. It's a barbed-wire fence, but also electric. You probably passed my car up the way, there— I'm just headed back to Pantherville to call a tow truck."

On the driver's-side seat was a tray of mail.

"But if you'd rather not give me a ride I completely understand," I said. "I'll just be moving on now."

I started walking, shakily. I had gone only a few steps when the Wagoneer stopped again alongside me. "You can ride," the woman said.

She was a young woman, perhaps twenty-five, with walnut-brown hair and fair skin with some freckles. Her manner was shy. Her face made me think of the face of a proboscis monkey with its long and not very delicate nose and curious blinking eyes, which is not to say that others would make the same association. She watched me climb in. This was in itself a tricky matter, because the Wagoneer had not been modified for passenger-side driving. The mail carrier sat on one hip on the inside edge of the passenger seat, extending her left leg over the drive-train hump while she steered with her left hand. I eased in under the mail tray with my knees cocked up against the door so that my feet would not interfere with her foot as it worked the floor pedals. She wore smallish black work boots and blue coveralls, and her hair was gathered behind her head in a beige rubber band.

On we went. Soon I was sweating heavily. It was hot inside the Wagoneer and I was wearing a wool tweed jacket that was too heavy for summer. There was no question of my getting out of it now, though, folded up and canted over as I was in my seat. I had not wished to leave the jacket in the Duster because its breast pocket contained my last two hundred and twenty dollars, along with a Visa credit card that I had sworn not to use.

"So this is East Tennessee," I said inanely. We passed a small clapboard house partly re-sided in tar paper and vinyl. In the front yard was a crape myrtle tree thickly burled on top from many seasons of pruning, and its trunk was painted solid white five feet up from the ground. Why?

"I've got to check the classifieds and find a place to rent," I said. "Did I mention that I just arrived?" I scrutinized the young female mail carrier. Her work kept her hands and foot busy, and she divided her attention between the tray of mail in my lap, the road in front of us, and the mailboxes where we stopped. There was a tub of advertising flyers in the floor on her side where she reached, without looking, at every stop. When there was outgoing mail she dropped it into a container behind my seat. She gave no answer to my question.

Her shyness did not surprise me much. My reading had prepared me to expect it from the natives of East

Tennessee. Consider what sort of a people, historically, would choose to settle in such a narrow-valleyed and rocky-soiled region. The gregarious, the lovers of openness, the public-minded, and also anyone who hoped to own or be associated with a large plantation would have kept on going, drawn to the fertile flat basin and plain of Middle and West Tennessee. The ones who stayed here were the ornery types: the clannish, the inward, the independent. Their farms were small enough to be worked by single large families without servants or slaves. They grew corn and tobacco, killed a hog or two in fall, and shot the anvil on election day. Indeed, the spirit of this region was distinct enough that Andrew Johnson had once proposed splitting off the eastern counties of Tennessee into a state of their own, to be called "Frankland." His reasons for suggesting this name are not known. He was a poor speller, and it is possible that he meant to name the state after the nation's first postmaster, Benjamin Frank*lin*. At any rate, nothing came of it.

"I have just driven in from New York City," I said by way of conversation. "Have you been to New York City?"

She shook her head no. I had guessed that, but wanted to make the point of not assuming.

"Mm, you should visit," I said. "There's no reason to be scared of the place. Millions live there. They walk fast, and you have to walk fast too, or be walked into. Just keep it moving or you'll get a shove. You might get shoved by an award-winning playwright or a multilingual UN employee, or then again by a homeless person who's in a hurry somewhere. Here's something to think of. True, it is the 'City that doesn't sleep,' but what is the corollary?"

Our eyes met briefly. "I don't understand what you're saying," she said.

"If it's true that the city is never completely asleep, then it's also true that the city is never completely awake. Many New Yorkers don't rise until two or three in the afternoon, you see. Some chefs, for example."

The tray in my lap was empty now. It was made of a milky white corrugated plastic. She lifted it from one end and shot it towards the back window of the Wagoneer, where it bumped the glass then landed in a stack of trays. Using both arms she set a full tray in its place across my legs. She wore no makeup, and it would not have surprised me to learn that she never had worn any in her life. Her face was not colorless, though. Her lips were pink and there were blotches of color that came and went on her throat. I noted her plump, dark brown irises.

"Perhaps there will be a postal convention one day that will give you an excuse to visit," I said. "One thing you will notice immediately if you walk around the city is that New Yorkers are constantly throwing out good furniture. This is because they live in such tiny apartments. They just don't have the room. If you ever should move to New York"—I smiled at her—"don't bother moving your furniture. Just bring your hand truck, and take it on a walk when you get there. You'll find chairs, dressers—"

"Where are you from originally?" she said.

"I beg your pardon?"

"Where are you from before New York?"

"What makes you think I'm not a native New Yorker?"

"Are you?"

"No, I'm not. I lived for varying periods in Florida, Texas, Scotland, and Ohio."

"How long did you live in New York?"

"Six months. The rents are very high."

"My cousin has a place he wants to rent," she said.

"I'll have to shop around," I said.

She had pulled up a one-lane dead-end road, and she stopped at the only house on it. After depositing some flyers and a magazine in the mailbox, she pulled from the smaller box next to it a newspaper and held the paper out to me.

"What is this?" I said.

"This is how we spread the news in Tennessee," she said quietly. She reversed into the gravel driveway and pulled out going back the way we had come. By the time I understood what was happening, we were back on the main road, and I was holding someone else's newspaper.

"You just took this from that box," I said.

"You said you needed to shop around," she said. She smiled.

It was a Johnson City paper. I quickly scanned the classified section. I saw that I could easily rent an entire trailer park for the amount per month I had paid Mrs. Chouri in Brooklyn. In spite of the many uncertainties of my present situation, I was so relieved to be out of New York I could have cheered.

But I didn't. First I had something important to do. "Please let me out," I said.

"Here?"

"Right here, please. I'm going to return this newspaper."

I spoke sharply, which seemed to frighten her a little. I hadn't meant to do that, and the expression of worry in her eyes gave me a sudden twist in my gut. But I would not be a party to the antisocial activity of newspaper stealing. "Excuse me, but I have some strong feelings about people and their subscriptions," I said, more mildly now. "I subscribe to a large number of journals myself, and the idea of walking out to my mailbox and finding my periodical gone, stolen, is upsetting to me. I don't like it."

"I wasn't stealing it," she said.

"Well, borrowing—but I won't go in for that either, for a simple reason that I will express to you in one word: time-sensitive. That is the nature of news, and this paper must be returned right now."

She had stopped the Wagoneer in the road, and I got out and laid the tray of mail across the seat. "You probably don't want to be giving rides on the job anyway," I said. "You're carrying the U.S. Mail."

She stared at me with her chin hanging down like a mailbox door. Something in me wanted to reach out a finger and flip it shut. But it closed by itself. The woman's throat was red.

"Well then," I said. "I do thank you for the thought, however." I felt awkward, as though I had not just spoken my mind. I thought I had spoken my mind. If it was not my mind, what was it then?

Without another word the mail carrier leaned towards me, grabbed the door, and swung it shut. She drove away.

3

To walk half a mile in the heat to return a stolen newspaper was a vexing digression. I was tempted to cut through what looked like an easily passable lot of trees, but I thought better of that and trudged onward, up the steep one-lane dead-end marked Jasper Price Road.

I returned the paper to its box then knocked on the front door, hoping someone might be home to let me use the telephone. No one answered, and I backed up into the yard to look around me. The house was tan brick with a small concrete porch and a second story added at the far end. The carport was heavily cluttered with houseplants, paint cans, some plastic Wise Men, and a car engine on a green shower curtain, among other things.

Under a bird feeder some small chickens were scratching the ground. I called out, "Hello?" A number of dogs began barking from behind the house, and I left.

This time I cut through the woods. I shed the tweed

jacket and folded it over my arm, not wanting to snag it on something. I was proud of the jacket. It was made by a venerable New York "bespoke" tailoring firm called Osim Lowe. I was myself not actually the bespeaker of it, but had bought it secondhand. It fit me well, however. I sometimes wondered about the person for whom it was made, and whether he was still alive.

You need good clothes to be taken at all seriously in the city. Perhaps this is not always true. I am told that bad clothes may be good depending on how they are worn and by whom, and at what moment. This is an example of the sort of bewilderment into which one plunges oneself, when exchanging a comfortable existence in the middle of the continent for a new life alone in New York.

True, I had been around some, living in several states and one foreign country while my mother went through her second, third, fourth, fifth, sixth, seventh, and eighth husbands. I got my education in the public schools, plus seven semesters at Sardis College, forty miles outside Cleveland. That first fall, Mother lived in an apartment at the edge of campus; then she married Tom DeWeese, my comma-splicing Composition Two instructor, and joined him in the leaking dome house which he had built himself. Mother was and is a die-hard optimist. As for DeWeese, he was the sort who makes a point of grading papers in green ink instead of red, because green is "the go color." His idea of teaching English composition was to arrange the desks in a circle and invite us to talk about "a time when I questioned authority." When conversation lagged, as it did, he would lapse into tales of his jug band days in the Pacific Northwest. He had suffered serious bruising on his fingertips while learning to play the doghouse bass. He ought to have spent less time spinning yarns, and more time caulking his dome house.

At Sardis I tried to make the best of a very imperfect situation. I attended on a full academic scholarship, quite an honor as I at first supposed, until I began to discern some disturbing things about my paying classmates. Though they were bad students generally, none of them ever failed a course. Some were dyslexic, some had addictions; many were childhood felons who'd had offenses such as manslaughter and prescription forgery expunged from their records. Then again, others were earnest but dim-witted. Sardis College, formerly one of the better small colleges in Ohio, had begun its decline. A few promising students like myself were enticed with scholarships, but most of the slots were sold off to the underachieving rich. Parents willingly paid the inflated tuition because Sardis had become a school where no one failed. When I confronted Tom DeWeese with this accusation he cheerfully admitted that he had not given a grade below C in years.

"You're a fraud," I told him.

"Lighten up, sonny boy," he said. He'd been using that term since marrying my mother.

"Never call me that again!" I said.

"What familial appellation would you prefer?"

He had a voice that was absurdly deep for a man of his size. I told him "Shut up," then blacked out in his office.

A complicated series of events ensued, culminating in the college nurse's attempt to persuade me that I was a victim of "social anxiety disorder." She accompanied this diagnosis with some very unpleasant insinuations regarding my family background. It was hogwash, but no one likes to have that sort of thing said about himself or his mother. The insinuations could not be disproved, but I did demonstrate that she was wrong about the social anxiety by taking a summer job selling fruit door-to-door. No person with a pathological anxiety in social situations could have sold as much citrus as I did to absolute strangers in their homes. That is not to say I enjoyed that job.

After Sardis I put in two weeks as a substitute teacher in the Cuyahoga County Consolidated School District before being hired to the position of managing editor of *Civil War Days* magazine, based in Galena, Ohio. The editor was Terence Choate, a tall, sleepy, and agreeable gray-headed man. He did not bring a great deal of energy to his work, preferring instead to let business lope along at a summertime pace throughout the year. Strong coffee had no effect on him. He was a friend to the amateur historian, whose substandard product he received with indulgence and often relied on to cheaply fill up the pages of our magazine.

Civil War Days was my home for six years, professionally that is. It was a comfortable home. There were always some crisp pages to shuffle, and I was often called on to chase down some lost fact or quotation, a task that I enjoy. My pay allowed me to maintain a small apartment and my journal subscriptions, which I coordinated with those of my friend and frequent dinner partner Shirley Walls, a Galena native. We sometimes divided a bottle of wine. These were modest but reliable pleasures.

Then one day I quit *Civil War Days* and left for New York. The decision was abrupt and not well thought out, but I had the sense that life was slipping away without my having fully engaged it. I worried that I had not been ambitious enough. My talents were limited, and I knew there was a timorousness in my nature for which I sometimes overcompensated. On the other hand, it seemed to me that it was time to do something. I hoped to find employment with one of the more prestigious general readership reviews such as the *New York Belletrist* or the *New Echelon*.

And then, there I was: one more beginner in the big city. How to start? Head-on was all I knew, but the *Belletrist* refused to buzz me in the door. From there I went to the offices of the *New Echelon*. I stood outside on Broadway watching people enter and leave. I was wearing an ordinary blue shirt and a gray sweater vest with pills on it. I left and threw the sweater away, and I acquired the Osim Lowe. The next day I presented myself and was buzzed in wearing the tweed jacket and clutching in my fingers the manuscript of an article examining the earliest published works on the life of Andrew Johnson. My article was not biography, but what I called biographiography. "I would like to speak directly with an editor," I said.

"In reference to what?" the male receptionist asked.

"In reference to this essay, which I wrote and would like to submit today for publication." I held it up for him to see.

He slid an envelope across the large desk. "We accept unsolicited subscriptions by mail," he said.

"In that case I would like to apply for employment now."

"Here? Doing what?"

"Any job at all," I said. "What is considered entry level?"

"Receptionist," he said.

Eventually I found a job in Brooklyn tending a spit-roaster—a job that, while not as simple as it may sound, is nonetheless not very complicated. Nobody had read my essay. I spent long days watching the lamb turn, thinking and planning, trying to profit. I thought of Andrew Johnson, who as a young tailor in Greeneville had hired a man to read to him from the newspaper as he sewed. I mentioned the idea to my employer, and the next day he brought in his wife to read aloud from a Greek newspaper, in Greek.

I spent most of my evenings at the New York City Public Library, a fine institution which is not however known as a major resource for Johnsonists. I had a special interest in the Johnson scrapbooks, which were kept up for many years. Andrew Johnson was never much for writing: he left no memoirs, and his letters are seldom reflective. He often closed letters "with apologies for this scrawl." But he preserved notes and clippings of every kind and gave strict instructions to his family that no piece of writing in his house ought ever to be destroyed. He had a reverence for the written word that was probably connected, at the psychological level, with his own struggle as a young man to become literate. He was a janitor's son, and he remains the only American president never to have had one day of schooling.

But the scrapbooks were mostly held in the Tennessee state archives, where they were difficult for me to gain access to for the embarrassing reason that I had no real credentials as an historian—not even a bachelor's degree. Sardis College had shut its doors over Christmas break my senior year. Its accreditation had been suspended. After three and a half years studying on scholarship, I left with a worthless transcript, and my dream of pursuing graduate study in history was also shot. It was a very grave disappointment for me. Perhaps only Tom DeWeese suffered as badly that Christmas, since he lost not only a job but a wife as well, when my mother divorced him.

But here is an instance in which I did manage to profit from a very unpromising situation. The only materials remotely connected to Johnson in the New York City Public Library's Special Collections were some boxes of manuscript pages and a few odd letters left behind by a man named Winfield S. Lewis, an aide to Governor Tilden who had written an early, inaccurate biography of Johnson for a book called *Avatars of the Democracy*. The book included chapters on a half-dozen deceased figures from the Democratic Party, and its purpose was transparently political: Lewis was a party hack, and not a subtle one. As biography his book was useless to historians, and it had been ignored almost since its publication in the 1880s. What I discovered, though—with a thrill that made my heart race—was that Lewis's correspondence could be of very great use because of what he had chosen to hide. Specifically, there was reference to one volume among the scrapbooks—"the sewn folio in the purple cover"—which Lewis had advised Johnson's daughter to destroy. She had refused, of course, but with assurances that the purple book would be carefully guarded from "antagonists to my father's name." My hope was that the book had been preserved down to this day, in a place where Johnson scholars had never found it.

This was why I had come to Tennessee. The lost purple book might well be near. I stopped walking to let that thought settle over me for a moment.

I was in a small, grassy clearing there in the woods, and I noticed that my shoe had come untied. I fixed that and then, observing a habit formed in the distant past, I untied the other shoe and retied it as well. They were wing tips, half a year old, and this was their first trip into the woods.

The grass here was freshly trimmed, I noticed. That struck me as odd. I couldn't see the road. It appeared that my shortcut had come out long.

"That's what happens," I said out loud to myself in the woods. The thoughts of my Johnson lead had made me cheerful, and I repeated the phrase in my Bob Dole voice.

I had started back on my way when a small man

scrambled up from a hole in the ground in front of me. He grabbed a string trimmer from behind a tree and pulled the starter cord. The motor sputtered then caught, and it droned high and loud. He raised the string trimmer and brandished the spinning string head at me.

"Don't come any closer!" he said.

4

I WAS GLAD NOT TO come any closer. I had not intended to. I would have been even happier to be farther away.

"What do you want out here?" the man yelled over the whine of his string trimmer.

"I'm cutting through to the road!" I said. "I was just returning a newspaper!"

"What?" He let the trimmer engine idle so he could hear me. "Say again?"

"I said I was returning the newspaper!" I pointed over my shoulder. "Someone borrowed it for me!"

"That don't sound right. I don't believe you!" He raised the trimmer head and throttled it up again.

He was a slight man, not tall, dressed in overalls with no shirt under them, and he had a light strapped onto his forehead. The trimmer engine was piercing and loud, but not so loud that I couldn't also hear the whirring of the heavy plastic line as he waved the trimmer at me with a cobralike swaying motion. A whipping from that string head might not be deadly like a cobra bite, but it would sting and leave welts.

"Who sent you?" the little man demanded.

"Nobody sent me! I'm new here!"

"Well I know you're new! Kind of warm in that coat, I'd say!"

Involuntarily I touched my breast pocket, where the cash was.

Seeing my hand move, he lowered the trimmer and let it idle again. "Hey, what have you got in there?" he said.

"Nothing," I said. This was some irony, I thought: I had gotten safely out of New York only to be mugged in the woods of Tennessee.

The man stared at my arm, which was frozen across my chest, with the thumb just under the lapel of my jacket. Abruptly he switched off the engine and laid the trimmer on the ground at his feet. "Don't shoot," he said quietly. He raised both hands.

I experienced a tingling sensation in my extremities, accompanied by a tinselly efflorescence in my brain. I smelled an odor like hot metal shavings. The experience is difficult to describe, but it was one I knew immediately. It went on for some seconds while my vision grew dark, and then I blacked out.

It was the first of these episodes I'd had since college. Years earlier, in elementary school, the attacks had been frequent. They'd come at moments of a particular kind of stress—once when my friend dropped his lunch tray in the cafeteria, for example, and once when the teacher's blouse popped open during story time. Often no one knew what had happened. I might remain perfectly motionless and upright in a quiet stupor until the spell had passed. Sometimes I was found out, as on one occasion when the seizure hit during a baseball game. I had gotten to first base, which was unusual for me, and my mother in her excitement shouted out a colorful expression not commonly used at public events involving children. I was carried from the field still frozen in my lead-off stance.

The humiliations of one's boyhood are best left unexamined, I think. The next thing I was aware of, there in the woods, my hand was being licked. I did not know by whom. I hadn't moved. I heard the small man's loud voice. "I believe him to be in a medical zombie state," I heard him saying. "Wait, he moved. I will call you back."

The man stood close to me, sliding a cell phone into a narrow pocket on the thigh of his overalls. The strap-on light was gone from his forehead now.

"Brownie, heel," he said.

A dog jumped to his side.

"I know who you are," the man said.

"You do?"

"Mm-hm. You're that boy whose yellow car died."

"That's right," I said. "How did you know?"

"I just know it. We don't get a lot of New Yorkites through here, okay?"

"I'm not actually a New Yorkite," I said. "I only lived there six months."

"Where are you from before that?"

"Florida, Texas, Scotland, and Ohio."

"All over. I see." He took a step back and looked me up and down. "You're interested in my dogs?"

"What? Not really," I said. I held my hand up and swallowed. I didn't feel good. A wave of dizziness came over me and I sat down cross-legged in the grass.

"Here's an offer," the man said. "I will let you take this dog home today for five hundred dollars, cash."

I considered the dog. It was a hound type, white with brown patches, wearing an orange reflective collar. Its saliva was drying on my wrist. The dog looked at me with its long wet tongue lolling out of its mouth, then looked up at the man.

There was some kind of misunderstanding here. "No thank you," I said.

The man squinted at me. "Are you *quite* sure?"

"Yes I'm sure. I don't want your dog." My jacket felt askew. I checked my pocket—the money was still there. "Did you frisk me?"

He shook his head thoughtfully. "If you knowed the first thing about treeing dogs you would have wanted to buy this old girl." He knelt and arranged Brownie so that she stood with her side to me. He tapped the insides of her rear legs to make her stretch them out, and he held up her tail by the tip. "Isn't she pretty?"

"The dog's looks are okay," I said. "How did you know who I am?"

"Dweena told me," he said. He tapped the pocket that held the cell phone. "Do you need to see a doctor?"

"No. This is something that has happened to me before."

"No need to explain," he said. "I've seen goats do a similar thing. Fainting goats."

We studied each other quietly for a few seconds.

"Listen, I have a place you might want to rent," he said.

His face was lean and had a surprised look. His hair was in a short crew cut and he appeared to be around thirty years old. "What were you doing in that hole?" I asked him.

"What hole?"

"The hole you were in when you surprised me. The hole you climbed out of."

He winced. "People don't need to know about that hole," he said.

"What's in it?"

"Me, when I'm letting my dogs run." I stood up and followed him over, and he shone the battery-powered light into the opening. An aluminum ladder led down about nine feet to what appeared to be a blue sofa on the cave floor.

"Why is there a sofa down there?" I said.

"It's not a sofa, it's a futon." He took some tobacco from a round canister and put it behind his lip.

None of this made sense to me, and I was shaky and disoriented from the blackout. I was also ravenous. I had eaten some Little Debbies in my car that morning and nothing since. "I need to get some food," I said.

He led me out of the woods and across the road to the

tan brick house. There was a plastic patio set on the carport amid the clutter, and he told me to have a seat. He propped his string trimmer by the door and removed his boots, then went inside. He was back shortly with a plastic jug, two cups, a grease-spotted paper bag, and a roll of paper towels. He laid everything out on the table then tore open the paper bag, which had fried chicken in it.

"Help yourself. Take whatever piece you prefer," he said.

I took a thigh. My hands were trembling, and I was salivating like a fiend.

"You're not very much of a dog man, are you?" he said.

"I'm not a dog man at all," I said with chicken in my mouth.

"I didn't think so. I could tell it from your lack of interest in Brownie. That was a test, see. I had a man offer me fifteen hundred for her this very week, and all I can say about that is, he was not in shouting distance."

I nodded. The thigh I was eating was greasy and very delicious. I could tell by the dampness of the crust that it had been reheated in a microwave oven.

"So then I knowed you wasn't a spy," he said.

"You thought I was spying on your dogs?"

"No, I'm saying I *knowed you wasn't.*"

He sat with a paper towel spread in his lap, holding a chicken breast. His chair faced out into the driveway and yard.

He turned suddenly and introduced himself. "Boo Price," he said.

I wiped my hand on a paper towel and we shook. "John Tolley."

"John, I'd like to rent you this house."

"It's much bigger than I need," I said.

"Not this one. This other one."

"How do you know I need to rent a house?"

"I told you, Dweena told me."

"Who is Dweena?"

"The one that give you the ride," he said.

"Oh." I was still confused. "Where is this other house?"

"Up on the knob." He pointed backwards over his shoulder. "You can't see it from here."

"I've got to have something cheap," I said.

"I can't take less than ninety dollars a month."

Well, that was cheap. I took a chicken leg and bit into it.

"And that includes your water," he said.

"The first thing I have to do is get my car towed."

"You and me can tow that little thing with no trouble," he said. He nodded at the pickup in his driveway, black except for one door that was green.

"I can't sign a long-term lease," I said.

"No lease. Pay cash."

"How near are we to Greeneville?"

"Purt near, as they say."

It occurred to me then that I had possibly misunderstood something. "Do you know, the reason I came back here was to return that newspaper," I said. "I thought she had stolen it."

"She told me about that," Boo Price said.

"But she didn't steal it, did she?"

"No. It's hers and mine," he said.

"I'm afraid I owe Ms. Price an apology. I had no idea she was the lady of the house."

He asked me if I wanted to have a look at the house on the knob.

"There's no need," I said. "I'll take it."

"Don't you want to see it first?"

I shook my head. I was anxious to have something settled, and I knew it couldn't get any cheaper than three dollars a day. Plus he had offered to save me a tow bill.

"How the place looks is not important," I said. "Is it out of the way?"

"Very."

"Then it's perfect. The reason I'm here is to work: to study, learn, and investigate. I'll be spending many hours in the local courthouses."

"We don't want any trouble, now."

"No. I mean I will be studying records in the courthouses. I'm a historian. An aspiring one, anyway."

"All right, John. I'll tell old Dweena you're not as bad a fellow as she said you was."

"I appreciate that, Boo. You've both been extremely welcoming."

"I hope you won't mind relieving yourself outdoors."

5

Boo took me in his truck to recover the Duster, and we towed it to Mark's Repair in Pantherville. Mark said, "Where'd you get that yellow paint?"

"It came with the car," I said.

"That is not Chrysler paint," he said.

We left it there. I gave Boo my first rent payment, prorated for the remainder of the month, and then it was time to settle in to my new quarters.

The house was on a hill up a pair of ruts past the end of the pavement on Jasper Price Road. It was a double-pen log house, sheathed in weatherboard—a classic of East Tennessee vernacular architecture. Boo assured me that this specimen, built by his ancestors, had been standing since before the Civil War. The roof was metal, rusted brown, and white paint dropped from the outside walls in meaty chips, like bacon bits.

The two main downstairs rooms were large, but with low, beamed ceilings and rolling floors. There was no straight line to be found in this house, and no square angle. The logs had been covered on the inside with tongue-and-groove boards, and the walls were a foot thick. The kitchen had metal cupboards and a double porcelain sink with draining boards. The refrigerator was dark and warm inside. "We'll have the power board out tomorrow," Boo said. He left me two jugs of water.

A path led from the kitchen door to an outhouse under a walnut tree. A little ways farther was the base of a hundred-foot steel tower carrying high-voltage transmission lines. I could see the lines stretching off for some distance in both directions, downhill with the trees and brush shaved away in a track beneath them. They were part of the famous Tennessee Valley Authority system, fed by coal plants and hydroelectric dams. The lines over the house gave off a steady buzzing noise, clearly audible from the back doorstep.

I turned in early on a sheetless daybed in the front room. The mattress was covered in textured tartan vinyl. I slept hard and was awakened early by pounding at the door. It was the man from the power board, backlit in the door glass by morning sun.

His work did not take long. He pushed a clear-globed meter head into a socket on the side of the house, and then he stepped onto the porch and averted his face to insert the main fuse.

He watched it for some seconds before turning to look at me. "This is a sixty-amp service," he said.

I told him I didn't know what that meant.

"We call it 'obsolete,'" he said.

"Is it dangerous?"

He gave a sigh. "That would be for an electrician to tell you. All I have to say is, never substitute fuses! Always use the *right* fuse."

I followed him into the house. Cringing slightly, he threw a wall switch. The switch made a loud snap, and the overhead light came on. We looked at the cloth-wrapped cables that were stapled along the walls and ceiling.

"Wired by farmers," he said. Then he left.

I tried the water and still the faucet was dry. I hiked down the hill to the Prices' place. Dweena Price was out delivering mail, but Boo was home watching a dog video. He invited me in.

We cut through the laundry room and kitchen into the living room. There was a pair of windows with the curtains drawn, and in front of these the television sat on an air hockey table between stacks of folded laundry. Boo slid over an armrest into the seat of a worn, plush recliner. "Look here," he said, pointing at the screen.

At first I couldn't tell what was happening. The camera bounced, and objects flashed out of darkness, lit by a harsh pale green light. I heard running footsteps and loud breathing, and then the camera stopped on the straightened back of a dog leaping against a tree trunk. The dog let out a strange, rapid cry that was not a bark, and not like anything I had heard before.

The light swung up into the branches. A fat, glassy-eyed raccoon looked down.

"Is that not something?" Boo said.

"What's wrong with the dog?" I said. "Is he hurt?"

"He's not hurt. He's never been happier."

"Why is he wailing?"

"Well that's how this dog lets us know that he treed," Boo said. "That's the sound we *listen* for."

"I see. And you listen from your cave?"

"Right. The cave is my *listening station.*"

"Is it safer down there?"

"Not really," Boo said.

"Why do coon hunters listen from caves?"

"Most of them don't, John. That's something unusual that I do."

He walked back up to the knob with me. He showed me the well pump, housed along with the air-bladder tank in a waist-high cinder-block structure. With the metal lid propped up over our heads, Boo jiggled the wires on the well pump, and then we went to the porch and checked the fuse box. The pump fuse was burned out. He took the fuse down the hill to find the correct replacement.

I sat down on the porch steps to compose a quick letter to my mother, who at this time was living in Pacific Grove, California, with her husband of nine months, Bill Zimmer. I had met him once, at their wedding, which he flew me out for, business class. It was a nice gesture but part of the deal, I suspect. Zimmer's children had the usual wariness towards me. They were polite enough, once they'd ascertained that I did have a job somewhere. They didn't want me feeling too at home in that spare bedroom.

They needn't have worried. I wouldn't have stayed as long as I did if Mother hadn't insisted I come early to be fitted for a tuxedo. Over the years, it has gotten harder for me to disguise the contempt that I feel for my mother's husbands, and I find the best thing is for me to stay far away from them. This current one, Zimmer, had a penchant for short pants and knee socks. It was his credit card that I'd been carrying in my jacket. Mother claimed he had told her to send it to me in case of emergency.

In the letter I gave her the basics of my new situation, including Boo's phone number should she need to reach me quickly. The log house did not have a phone. I also gave her a short account of my visit to the National Mall in Washington and an extended evocation of the scenery and atmosphere of Upper East Tennessee, along with my usual request that she save the letter in case I should want to use parts of it in a future work. Boo returned with the same fuse, but he had carefully wrapped the copper base of it in aluminum foil. He screwed it in and we heard the pump start. "This is doing it hillbillywise," he said.

I asked him would it not be a fire hazard, doctoring a fuse that way.

"I've done it this way my whole life," he said. "My daddy done it this way, too. Does this house look like it's ever burnt down?"

"No."

"Does my house down the hill look like it ever burnt?"

"No, it doesn't."

"And when this house does burn, it's *my* problem."

"It's my problem too, if I'm asleep in the house when it's burning."

"Well, just know your exits, and let me worry about the rest. I'm a fireman, John."

"A real fireman?"

"Yes, real. I'm on call as we speak." He showed me a beeper from the chest pocket of his overalls. It was labeled "PVFD" in red plastic label tape.

We went into the house and found water running across the floor of the front room. Boo ran to the kitchen and yelled for me to shut the pump off. I ran to the porch, but I was scared to touch the fuse. In a minute Boo came running onto the porch. He unscrewed the fuse, and the pump stopped.

"What happened?" I said.

"Pipes is burst," Boo said. He frowned. "I need to see a man about a dog."

"You know where the facilities are," I said.

He stared at me. "I'm meeting him in town," Boo said. "You come too, and we'll buy you some pipe to fix this mess."

6

BOO DROPPED ME OFF at the tiny Pantherville Post Office, where I held the door for a woman and her two children, letting them go in first though I had arrived before them. Most people don't like waiting in line; I don't like to have people waiting behind me. When my turn came I told the clerk, a large-headed, dull-looking man, that I wished to rent a post office box.

He swiveled his large head and called in a loud, reedy tenor, "Dwayne!"

Several seconds went by while we waited. The clerk passed the time silently, looking into his lap.

At length a man emerged from the back. He was perhaps sixty years old, tall and heavily built, with curly, lead-colored hair. His name tag said "Dwayne Loupe, Postmaster." He asked me mildly, "Can I help you?"

I told him I wanted to rent a post office box, and he gave me a form and left. The form required the names of all persons who would receive mail at the box. I listed thirteen names and handed the form to the big-headed clerk.

"Dwayne!"

A woman in a long T-shirt with no pants visible got in line behind me. She was holding a large carton that touched her chin. An elderly woman followed her, carrying a purse, a change purse, a tissue, and an envelope. One of the women smelled strongly of baby powder.

The postmaster came again and took my form from the clerk. He scrutinized it then asked me, "What is your relationship to all these other people?"

I explained, somewhat reluctantly, that those were made-up names under which I subscribed to various magazines.

"Are they blue magazines?"

"No. They're cultural and academic journals."

"Why the aliases, then?"

"Isn't that my business only?" I said.

"It's suspicious," the woman with the carton said.

The postmaster studied her bare legs. I chose to ignore her. Then I chose to turn around and invite her to skip ahead of me in line.

"I'd be most glad to," she said. "Your project may take a while."

"Let's get this settled first," the postmaster said. "Who is this Mr. Lancelot Quinny?"

"He's not a real person. That's the name under which I subscribe to a magazine called *The Loquat*."

"What is Mr. Quinny's nationality?"

"He doesn't have one. He's made up."

"And Mr. Pom Nodore? Or is that Ms.?"

"I don't know," I said. "Mr., I guess."

"You don't know?"

"It doesn't matter," I said.

"It matters to Pom Nodore."

"I'd say it does," the lady with the box said. She and the other woman got to cackling. Even the big-headed clerk cracked a simple grin.

"Pom Nodore—*gender uncertain*," the postmaster said. He wrote a notation on the form. "Barry Mounts—*Mr.*" He made a note. "Lucille Bismarck—that's a *Ms.* Montgomery Formulus—*Mr.*, I presume." He went on down the list, which continued onto the back of the form, adding the courtesy title alongside each invented name.

"Please give me back my form and I will apply somewhere else," I said. I was beginning to smell metal shavings.

"We'll not have that!" the postmaster said. "Why, this list alone almost doubles the ranks of our in-office boxholders. It means a bump up in appropriations, and an eventual salary hike for yours truly. For now, you owe us twelve dollars."

I paid, received my key, and left.

I crossed the road to the small grocery called the Pantherville Store. The shelves were almost bare, and not all of the overhead lights were on. A cashier with circles under her eyes watched me walk through the aisles. I purchased a dusty jar of Spaniard Brand instant coffee, a loaf of white bread, a box of cereal, some milk, and a jar of peanut butter—a small one because it was not my brand. I also got a handful of quarters. The tired cashier told me I would find a pay telephone a few steps up the road in front of the brown-brick building that housed the volunteer fire department and the local branch of the county public library.

I went there and fed eight quarters into the telephone. I dialed directory assistance and requested Nashville, then the switchboard for Vanderbilt University. "I am calling for the offices of the *Southern Historical Review*," I said.

The phone rang and a voice like sweet, dark gravy said, "Hello?"

"Hello. Is this the extension for the offices of the *Southern Historical Review?*"

"You have those offices," the voice replied.

"My name is J. Hynde Tolley," I said. "I'm calling to inform you that my address has changed."

"Hang on, please." There was a long silence, during which my quarters ran out and I inserted more. The gravy voice returned. "I don't find you on our roster," it said.

Guessing the problem, I said, "I think possibly you are looking at the roster of subscribers. I am calling to inform you because I have submitted an article to your journal." It was the Johnson biographiography I had carried all over Manhattan, which no one there would read. Despairing, I had sent it to the *SHR* as a last choice.

"Oh, you're a prospective contributor? Wait a minute—Hynde Tolley. Yes, I remember the piece."

"You've read it?"

"Why yes, the other day. It had sat, you know, under something else awhile. We get many submissions, as you may imagine. Plus, I'm just damned slow. That's the real issue."

"Am I speaking to Professor Van Brun?"

"You are, sir." The voice swelled to add, "I am Luke Van Brun."

I had expected a managing editor or perhaps a graduate assistant to pick up the phone. I had not expected the editor himself. "I am familiar with your book, *Andrew Johnson: Partyless President*," I said. "I own it and have—"

"You own it?"

"I have read it and often refer to it."

"Why that's so kind of you to do so," Van Brun said. "Where are you?"

"Well, I'm at a pay phone, at the moment."

"In town, though? I was going to suggest you come by today or Monday, so we could go over a few notes."

"Notes? You've made notes on my essay?"

"I have made a few notes. That's how I work, Hynde Tolley, and if you can't accept critique I can't work with you. Can you accept critique?"

"Yes. Do I understand that you may be interested, then?"

"That I may be when? Do you what? I don't know what you are saying."

"Are you publishing my article?"

"That is my intention. I wish to publish your article in

the *Southern Historical Review,* volume ninety, number two, winter theme issue. Assuming, that is, that you are willing to subject it to the cleansing fire of editorial scrutiny."

"Cleansing doesn't disturb me in the least," I said.

"Certain matters of style, plus some small issues of documentation. We'll speak Monday, then, midmorning, here in my office. You know where I am?"

"On the campus of Vanderbilt University?"

"You have it! Ask anyone to direct you. Now I must let myself go."

"Certainly. Monday, then."

"Monday!"

He hung up, and so did I. I replaced the receiver soundly, with a satisfying force.

Monday, midmorning!

I was hovering now, not standing. Would I ever need feet again?

I crossed the parking lot and knocked on the door of the Pantherville Volunteer Fire Department, where Boo had told me to meet him. No one answered, so I went inside. Across the dim, lodgelike lobby was a man on a sofa, half supine, watching television with the volume up high. I stepped up behind him, startling him badly. He twitched, and his bag of chips spun to the floor.

"Have you seen Boo Price?"

"He's at the Maisy!" the fireman said.

I had no idea what Van Brun could have meant by "small issues of documentation." I take the back seat to no one on documentation of sources. Some (Terence

Choate) had accused me of overdocumenting. But that was neither here nor there because *my career as a historian had begun*!

There was planning to do. I had so little cash: how much would a bus ticket cost? At the Maisy I set my groceries in the back of Boo's pickup and went inside, joining him at a table.

"John, let me ask you something," he said.

"Go ahead!"

"Gobbledygook."

I waited for more. He hadn't mumbled. He knocked back his cap with a knuckle so that it perched on the rear of his skull.

"I beg your pardon?"

"Gobbledygook, John."

I laughed. "I don't understand, Boo."

"Gobbledygook!" His arm shot across the table and he hit me smartly on the side of my head.

I grabbed the spot. My scalp was quivering. "Why did you do that?" I said.

"Look here," he said, pointing at me. "Because you didn't do just as I told you to do."

"I don't know what you're talking about!"

"You don't know what *gobbledygook* means?"

"No!"

"And how does that make you feel?"

"It makes me feel confused!"

"I would think so! And if it doesn't work with you, how's it going to work with a dog?"

"It wouldn't!"

"Right! And that's what I told that boy just now—*hitting the dog will not make him understand.* You know why? If that was the case I'd be the smartest man in the country, because I had my little ass whipped every second day all through school. But I think I come out just the same as I would have anyway, John."

A woman came to our table with a notepad.

"I'll have the cornbread and soup beans with onions on it, and sweet tea to drink," Boo said.

"Me too," I said.

The waitress left.

"Did you get all your errands took care of?"

"Yes, and now I have a new problem. I have to get to Nashville Monday morning for a meeting with an editor."

"Editor of what?"

I filled Boo in, explaining that the *SHR* was a respected history journal edited by Professor Luke Van Brun, a prominent Johnsonist of the generation prior to mine.

"Sounds important," he said.

"How can I best get to Nashville?"

"Hm. I was considering driving my truck there," Boo said.

"You were?"

"Yep. Ronnie broke his foot and needs chauffeuring to his session thing."

"I'd buy your gas if you'd let me ride along," I said.

He worked his eyebrows up and down. It was not an expression so much as an exercise. "Why in the world not?" he said.

"What crazy luck!"

All at once I was hungry. My mouth began to water profusely and even dribbled.

"The *SHR* is a journal of moderate to high importance," I said from behind a napkin. "I admit it's a specialized publication—not something for the general readership. It is held in all of the major research libraries."

"Hot dog," Boo said. "Good on you."

"Van Brun's opinion is rather highly regarded in my field."

Boo tilted his head and gave me a thoughtful nod.

The food came, and we leaned back from the table while the waitress set a yellow bowl in front of Boo and a light green one in front of me. The beans had large chunks of raw white onion on top, and the bowls were made of melamine, my favorite material to eat from. There was also a basket of steaming cornbread muffins and a little dish of butter pats wrapped in gold foil. We ate all of it, leaving no crumb nor smudge.

7

M ONDAY MORNING AT 3:30 ante meridiem I was
standing at the draining board in the little low-
ceilinged kitchen of my rented log house, assembling
sandwiches for the trip. The kettle went off, and I mixed
a thermos of Spaniard Brand. I packed the provisions
into a canvas zipper-bag along with a travel mug, a legal
pad, several unsharpened pencils, a small pencil sharp-
ener, and a fresh copy of my article.

I love setting out before dawn for a trip. Expectancy is
high, and thoughts with the lurid color of dreams crowd
the brain, but with an undreamy sharpness that is lent by
the first cup of coffee. In the quiet I imagined the following exchange:

LUKE VAN BRUN: Hello, Mr. Tolley. May I call you
Hynde?

J. HYNDE TOLLEY: You are welcome to, though my
friends hail me John.

LVB: John, then, certainly. Reading and rereading your essay, John, I find that I feel an affinity both deep and broad for the mind of its author. I gather you hold no postgraduate degrees.

JHT: Alas, no.

LVB: Of course. I was certain I sensed the vitality and uncontaminated perspective of the autodidact. Andrew Johnson himself—

JHT: Not a day of formal schooling.

LVB: And Lincoln had but little more! I am surrounded, here at Vanderbilt University, every day by the most prosperous and also some of the best-groomed young people of the Southeast region; yet I have often considered the pleasure it would be to pass along some of my learning to a student unprejudiced by privilege, uncoddled by the softnesses of a well-off childhood. I wonder whether you might be that diamond in the rough whom I have sought as my protégé, John.

Indulging in fantasy conversations is a harmless way to pass the time. It is one of the cheap pleasures. I wasn't ready to stop just yet.

LVB: I must say, John, it seems to me that in this paper you have hit upon an aspect of the Johnson record that has gone sadly underdiscussed by my colleagues. I wish that I had thought of it first, and beaten you into print! But of course, that is only a jest. Now let us decamp to the smoking

room and crack open this bottle of port. It has put
in some years on the rack, and I think you will
find it mature.

This last flourish about the port did embarrass me even
as I was enjoying it. There was no need for concocting
fantasy conversations anyway, because a real conversation would be taking place soon. What would Tom
DeWeese, Ph.D., say now? Had he ever been summoned
to the offices of the *Southern Historical Review* to discuss
a forthcoming contribution? Answer: *no*.

A new phase of my life was beginning. I thought with
a quick pang of my friend Shirley Walls in Galena—my
discussion partner and frequent dinner companion. I felt
a fondness towards her and some regret at the thought of
having broken up our two-person reading group. I hoped
she wasn't lonely. Like the port of my daydream, Shirley
had also put in some years on the rack. I wished her the
best. I decided I would send her a contributor's copy of
the *SHR* winter theme issue with the following note: "To
Shirley. A work like this must not hope for a wide audience, but it may hope for a perceiving one." She would
not miss the implication, which placed her among that
discerning group for whom my work was intended.

I hiked down the hill in bright moonlight, toting my
zipper bag. The high-voltage towers loomed against the
deep sky, emblems of the grand efficiency of human
effort. Down the hill Boo's carport light was on, and I
knocked at the door.

He was dressed in a terry cloth bathrobe, and he held

his head with one hand. "Printer's Alley will have to wait," he said. "I have a terrible migraine and can't go."

"A migraine?"

"An extremely bad headache," he said. He lowered his hand, uncovering a set of steel-framed eyeglasses with thick, bottle-green lenses. I hadn't seen these before. "Dweena's going to drive you," he said.

"Dweena?"

I heard a quiet sniff and looked past him into the kitchen. Dweena Price was kneeling on the tile, tugging at and then tying the lace of a heavy black work boot.

"Good night," Boo said. He walked away towards the back of the house.

Dweena stood up without looking at me. She gathered her dark hair behind her neck and snapped a rubber band around it.

"Good morning," I said.

She glanced at me and nodded quickly as she walked past.

I followed her outside onto the carport. "You're going to drive me all the way to Nashville?" I said.

But she had already gotten around to the far side of the Wagoneer and didn't hear me, or at any rate didn't answer.

I got in, glad at least to be riding on the passenger side this time. I shut the door, and immediately the Wagoneer started up and we were moving.

One thing had to be dealt with right away. "I apologize for my curtness the other day," I said. "I hope that Boo explained my misapprehension about the newspaper."

"That's okay," she said quietly.

I couldn't see her face well. I realized too late that offering my apology in darkness, or rather by a faint combination of moonlight and instrument panel light, made for a weird moment of unintended intimacy. I quickly faked a cough in order to break the spell. In the course of pretending to cough I inhaled some saliva, and the bogus coughing fit became a real one.

She looked straight ahead out the windshield. All I could make out was her profile, dominated by the roundish prominent nose. She had thick lips and a rather small chin. She sat very straight, I noticed—an unusual trait, these days, especially for a shy person.

"I do appreciate your taking the time to do this," I said. "You and your husband have both been very kind to me."

"Me and my what?"

"You and Boo."

"Boo is my *cousin*," she said.

Though it was dark, I put a hand to my face to hide my reaction. Married cousins! Of course I had seen that there was something off about this pair, but I had never guessed it was so bad. What bizarre Appalachian nightmare had the poor backward girl lived? At least there were no children!

"I live upstairs in the apartment," Dweena said. "We're not *married*."

"The apartment?"

"At the end of the house," she said. "There's a separate entrance."

"Oh! Of course. Yes, yes, yes. And you're *cousins*."

A long, loud snort came from the back seat just then. I jumped and let out a short cry.

"What is that?" I said.

"Ronnie Runnels," she said. "Are you awake, Ronnie?"

There was no answer.

"He spent the night back there," Dweena said.

"Why? Why? Who is Ronnie?"

"What is wrong?" she said quietly. "Why are you excited?"

"Ronnie startled me! Okay, I'm settling down." Wanting something to busy myself with, I took the thermos out of my zipper bag and poured some coffee. I offered Dweena a cup.

"I'll have some, but you don't need any," she said.

I gave her the travel mug and poured myself a cup in the flask lid. "And why is Ronnie sleeping in the back seat?"

"So I wouldn't have to get him out of bed at his house," she said.

"He's going to Nashville, too?"

"Yes. He's got some big vote today."

I remembered now that Boo had said he was chauffeuring someone to a "session thing" in Nashville. In my Tolleycentric universe that detail had held no special interest. Now I wondered, though. "He's not in the legislature, is he?"

"Yes," she said, looking down at her coffee.

"You're kidding." Discreetly I twisted to get a look

into the back. It was dark, but I thought now that I could smell him. "Which body?" I said.

"Is there more than one back there?"

"No, I mean which body of the legislature?"

"Oh. The House of Representatives."

"And he's from Pantherville?"

"Yes," she said.

"Why that's the same seat Johnson held from 1835 to 1837, and then again from 1839 to 1841! Well, not exactly the same, since the districts have been redrawn. But I suppose you know all this, being from here."

"I never followed it much," she said.

"Oh yes. Johnson's first elected post was as an alderman in Greeneville, and then he served as mayor. Then he went to the Tennessee House, and then the state Senate, and then the U.S. House. Then he served as governor of Tennessee, and then he served in the U.S. Senate, and then he ran for president and lost, and then Lincoln made him military governor of Tennessee, and then he was vice president, then president, and then he ran again for president and lost, and then he went back to the U.S. Senate before he died."

"I doubt Ronnie will make it that far," she said.

"And how are you and Boo acquainted with him? Are you old friends?"

"I work with Ronnie at the post office. He and my uncle are friends."

"Boo's father?"

"No, my other uncle. Boo's father died when he was in prison."

"Boo's father was in prison?"

"No, Boo was," she said. "He didn't tell you about that?"

"No."

"The backyard of the house you're renting used to be in marijuana and corn," she said.

"I see. What kind of corn?"

She turned to look at me. "Silver Queen," she said. She turned back towards the road. "What kind of coffee is this?"

"Spaniard Brand instant coffee. I bought it at the Pantherville Store. Would you like yours freshened?"

"No thank you," she said.

"Say the word when you do," I said. I refilled my cup.

"You know, anything you buy at that store could be decades old," Dweena said. "Did you check the expiration date?"

I hadn't. "The seal appeared to be intact," I said.

We rode quietly while the sky turned deep blue and the black mountains became visible against it. We were driving south on Interstate 81 towards the junction with 40, which would take us west over the Cumberland Plateau. I thought about the day ahead, and from time to time I noticed the stars. Fewer showed each time I looked.

There was another long snort from the back seat, followed by words spoken into a pillow.

"Ronnie? Do you need to stop?" Dweena said.

He didn't answer, but at the next exit she pulled off the freeway and into a BP station. We stopped by a pump, and I heard a blanket being whipped to the floor in back. I cleared my throat and turned around slowly to introduce myself. The legislator was already letting himself out, though. He crossed the parking lot hurriedly on a pair of crutches. He was wearing an orange nylon training suit.

I got out and went around to the gas pump, but Dweena had already started it and was cleaning the windshield. I stepped up and watched her. She was adept with the squeegee and left no lines.

"You're good at that," I said.

"Look there," she said.

She stopped squeegeeing and pointed towards the base of a steel post just beside the pump. I saw what I took to be a folded dollar bill attached to the side of the post, possibly taped there. I reached to take it and she caught my arm, and then I saw that the thing was not a folded dollar but a moth. Its wings, spread flat against the white paint, were three and one half inches across. We studied it awhile.

I went inside to pay for the gas and met Ronnie on his way out. I extended my hand. "My name is John Tolley," I said. "I've got coffee and sandwiches in my bag, and you are welcome to take the front seat, now that you're awake."

He blinked at me, then lowered his large head and looked at my hand. He didn't speak.

"I beg your pardon," I said. Of course he couldn't shake hands while he was holding a crutch. I backed up and held the door for him, and he made his way without a word. He was familiar to me, though I couldn't place him.

"You got snubbed," the clerk said.

"He has just woken up," I explained.

"Woken? You mean *waked*," the clerk said.

"I mean *woken*," I said.

Back at the Wagoneer, we resumed the same seating arrangement. Dweena twisted to look into the back. "Ronnie, where's your other crutch?" she said.

He looked into the floor. The Wagoneer was roomy, but there wasn't room to lose a crutch.

"You left it inside," Dweena said. "Run get it."

"Won't you run get it for me?" he said in a quavering tenor. The voice surprised me: it did not sound like the voice of an elected politician.

"Where you left it, I can't get it," Dweena said.

Ronnie got out and headed back for the building.

"I know that man," I said. "He's the clerk from the post office in Pantherville!"

She nodded yes.

That oboelike voice was unmistakable. Remembering our encounter, I marveled at the inaccuracy of my impression of him. He had struck me as a dullard.

"He rented me my post office box," I said.

"I heard all about that," Dweena said.

"You did? What did you hear?"

"I heard you had a list of strange aliases."

She stared at me. I couldn't read her.

"I was in a sort of magazine club with a friend in Ohio," I said. "An annotating club. I put these names on my subscriptions and she thought they were funny, you see. Humorous."

"You made them up?"

"Right. All except my own."

"Some of them weren't funny, like 'Barry Mounts.' What's funny about that?"

"*She* thought it was funny."

"You must have thought so too, if you made it up for her benefit."

I considered that. "I knew what would set her off," I said. "She had what I would describe as a hermetic sense of humor."

"What does that mean?"

"Hermetic: sealed off from the environment."

Dweena blinked slowly. "That seems a little sad," she said.

"Does it?" It hadn't seemed sad when Shirley was stomping up and down the hallway of her duplex apartment, shouting out "Hello, my name is Barry Mounts!" at the top of her voice repeatedly. It had seemed like a funny joke then.

Representative Runnels returned on both crutches and we got back onto the road. The sun came up and we reached Knoxville, the city that in 1796 had served as the first capital of the new state of Tennessee. I mentioned this fact out loud but no conversation resulted. Runnels had gone back to sleep.

The low morning sun scraped the roofs of downtown Knoxville with pinkish light. We passed among the upper stories of buildings, as the interstate was elevated here. I saw the tower with a gold-colored glass ball on top of it that was built for the 1980 World's Fair.

"It wasn't so long ago that Daniel Boone and his band

of ax-handlers cut their road through the woods to what is now Middle Tennessee," I said to Dweena. I spoke quietly, not wanting to wake Mr. Runnels. "Twelve men abreast, hacking their way through brush and vine. There were also thirteen dogs along. Am I boring you?"

"No. You're like a human Book on Tape."

"Hm. Time to flip me over," I said.

"What did you mean by that?"

"I don't know. I just said it."

"Listen," she said. "Boo doesn't really have a migraine."

"He doesn't? How do you know?"

"It was an excuse. He's afraid of trips."

"What do you mean, 'afraid of trips'?"

"He won't travel more than twenty-five minutes from the house. It scares him. He panics."

"Why?"

"I don't know why."

"Why did he offer to drive me to Nashville, then?"

She gave a shrug. "He wanted to help."

"He could have told me the truth this morning," I said.

"He was embarrassed," she said. "He couldn't even get his clothes on this morning. He was a mess when I got down there."

"A mess?"

"He was upset," she said.

I thought about that. It surprised me, but then when I thought some more it didn't surprise me as much.

"Everyone's different," Dweena said.

8

W E MADE GOOD TIME, and shortly after nine o'clock Dweena dropped me off at the campus of Vanderbilt University. Ronnie Runnels was still unconscious.

I stood awhile at the edge of a parking lot, looking in past rows of cars. Far away and above the campus rose the steel frame of a tall building in progress. The middle floors were closed in with pale yellow sheathing. Near the top an expanse of blue tarpaulin flapped in the air.

I started in. If there was a main entrance to the campus I had missed it, and after crossing a second and a third parking lot I found myself at the foot of a concrete loading dock behind a red brick building. There was a woman on a folding chair beside the back entrance, and I asked her the way into campus.

"You're on the campus," she said.

"Where is the middle of campus?"

"Go that way," she said, pointing.

"That's where I just came from," I said.

She hooked her arm in a horseshoe shape, still pointing.

I went back out of her sight then stepped over a low fence onto a bed of ivy and followed a series of empty bike racks past a cottage with a mossy roof and windows with bubbled glass. I was on a brick path now. I walked past a modern white science building with a glass foyer and then I fell in behind a small group of students and followed them until we rounded a turn and came to a large, open yard.

This was more like it. Darkened old college buildings of brick and stone enclosed the green on four sides. An elderly man ran by me in shorts, an elastic sweatband on his head. Above me on a branch, a squirrel chattered. A small plastic laminate sign was fastened to the tree trunk, engraved with the words *Quercus rubra.*

I crossed the square and entered the attractive and impressive Heard Library, the use of which is not however open to the public, as I learned when I knocked my femurs on the locking turnstile. From there I found my way to Rand Hall, where I browsed through a food court for some time before deciding on a plain biscuit. I wound up with a cheese omelet because I stood in the wrong line. I ate the omelet, then swished my mouth out with water and asked directions to the offices of the *Southern Historical Review.* A cashier looked it up in the campus directory.

The building housing the *SHR* had a floor of pink granite. I climbed a curving stairway and followed a long hall lined with office doors. At the end was room 211. The inhabitant's name was painted in black on a strip of brass. I knocked.

"Come in!" came the answer, and I did.

Professor Luke Van Brun stood at a bookcase behind a large desk. Windows in the far wall cast a milky light upon him. He was a big man, both tall and portly, with a bald head and eyes like small pans. His scalp was dull and spotted, with strips of sticky-looking hair at the sides, and he had a rather flat nose with flying nostrils. He held two books in each hand. He placed them into a cardboard box on his desk.

"I'm J. Hynde Tolley," I said. "We spoke Friday by telephone."

He looked me over from my head down, wordlessly and with no expression.

"You asked me here to go over my essay for the *Southern Historical Review*," I said.

His eyebrows fell a great distance. "Yes. Please sit down and pardon the disarray—I am preparing for a well-earned sabbatical," he said.

There were two chairs opposite the desk, one filled with books and the other holding a silver tea tray with potted succulents on it. I moved the books to a bare spot on the counter at the back of the office. The shelves above the counter were half empty, but journals were stacked knee-high along the floor.

Van Brun had paused to frown at something in a book. He flipped the page, flipped back two pages, then shut the book with a snap and blew along the top edge. He set the book into the cardboard box and then stepped around to the side of the desk, at which point I saw something which distressed me much more than it ought to have, which was that Luke Van Brun was wearing sandals. His feet—I will not describe them in detail but will simply say that they looked as though they had been used hard every day for six decades or more. And they had not been well maintained. They needed attention, *today.* It was all I could do not to throw up when I saw the horrible neglected feet of Luke Van Brun, and then he extended his hand to me. I clenched my jaw and shook it.

His smile was stained but ingratiating. To my relief, he moved behind the desk again to sit. He said, "Tolley, I love your essay. Significant, original."

"That's very kind of you," I said.

His gray-blue eyes, rather bleary, skidded over the furnishings of the large office. "Our fifteenth president has been all but ignored of late, and his role in delaying the war always bears further discussion."

"That is true," I said. "Buchanan is a fascinating figure."

"What was it we were meeting for?"

"To discuss the essay."

"Oh yes. Let's start right away."

"You said you wanted to run it in the *SHR*. Perhaps not the next issue but the one after. The winter theme issue, you said."

"And I do, exactly so. That is my intention, and I feel certain the members of my editorial board will concur. If not I shall resort to strong-arm persuasion."

"Well! You said you wanted to discuss some possible alterations."

"I did?"

"Documentation issues, you said. 'Small matters of style.'"

Van Brun laid his forehead into his hand. Then he raised his head suddenly, and then he massaged his eyes. "Prompt me with a few words regarding the substance of your essay," he said.

"It is a brief but comprehensive survey of early published works on the life of Andrew Johnson. A Johnson *biographiography*, if you will."

"A Johnson whaty whaty?"

"A history of Johnson books," I said. "Pre-1900."

Van Brun wiped his mouth. "I'm interested in the other one you sent, the one on Buchanan. Didn't you send an essay on Buchanan?"

"I didn't send an essay on Buchanan."

"I think you did. The one with the long footnote about his pants."

I shook my head no.

"You are P. Gordon McIlvane, correct?"

"My name is J. Hynde Tolley."

He looked down at his desk and picked up a paper from the top of a stack. "P. Gordon McIlvane," he said. "Why did I think you were he?"

"I certainly don't know," I said. "My essay concerns Andrew Johnson."

"Okay. Well, I'm not sure I've read that one. Are you quite sure you addressed the envelope correctly?"

"I did use care in addressing the envelope," I said.

"Maybe it hasn't reached me yet. How long ago did you send it?"

"Eleven weeks ago."

"It ought to have been here by now."

He looked around him at his office. There were many boxes, most with their flaps open. Books were stacked everywhere, and the desk was mounded over with papers, envelopes, mugs, a towel, a lamp, and a map that appeared to have been recently pulled from the wall. A thumbtack still clung to its hole in one corner, fixed there lightly by rust.

When Van Brun spoke again, his voice was smaller and softer. "You've caught me at a disorganized moment, Mr. McIlvane," he said.

"I understand," I said. "I'll simply check back with you later, when you've had time to read my submission."

"Yes. Well, that's good. But I will go ahead and tell you that it is possible, though not a certainty, that your paper was among a group of papers that has been mislaid. There was a set of them. They were damaged, actually. I'm damned embarrassed about it. You've heard the story of Carlyle and Mill, no doubt, when Mill's chambermaid destroyed the manuscript of *The French Revolution*. Carlyle had to write the damned thing over."

Of course I knew the story. I had heard it from Tom DeWeese when he and my mother returned from their honeymoon, in the course of which he had lost my term paper.

"Deeply embarrassed," Van Brun said, "and there

isn't much one can do about it. The manuscript was burned."

"My essay got *burned?*"

"No, Carlyle's did. Yours was water damaged. *Assuming* it was in that pile."

"Would you like another copy?"

"Yes. I insist that you send me one."

I took the fresh copy from my zipper bag and held it out to him over his mounded desk.

He waved his hand backwards and said, "Set it anywhere."

"I'll place it in your hand," I said.

He glanced at me, then took the essay.

I rose and left the office.

9

MY SHOE SOLES CLATTERED loudly on the polished granite. I went the wrong way and took some stairs that led up a bell tower. I came back down from the bell tower and found a men's room, where I washed my face at a heavy, small sink.

My intention was to feel nothing now. Once the chain reaction of feelings started, it would be difficult to stop. I pumped the soap dispenser, an old type with a glass globe and metal nipple. I made the mistake of glancing at myself.

In a furious spasm I smeared pink soap across the mirror, wiping out the reflection of my face. I accompanied this action with a stream of hissed obscenities.

The door creaked open and Van Brun stepped into the men's room. He froze on the tile in his sandals. We looked at each other and then he went on about his business.

I rinsed my hands. Trembling now, I dampened a paper towel and wiped the soap off of the mirror.

Van Brun, at the next sink down, said, "I'm off to get myself *eine Tasse Kaffee.* Care to join?"

I turned to face him. If there had been a way to slap his face without touching his face, I would have done it.

"Oh, I know you're angry," he said. The brown gravy quality had come back into his voice. "People are awful," he said. "This is just the sort of crap you have to deal with."

I told him that until recently I had been the managing editor of a magazine with a monthly circulation of twenty thousand copies, and I had developed a simple system in which new submissions were kept in a certain tray until they were acted on, and then the author was notified yes or no. It didn't take a great deal of intelligence, I said—only a bit of organization.

He slouched and took on an abstracted, guilty look. "Let me buy you a cup of coffee anyway," he said.

I followed him out of the building and into the brightness of day, which did nothing to improve his appearance. His trousers were of a velvety brown corduroy, sacklike in their dimensions and rubbed shiny at the seat and calves. His broad blue shirt had the shape, from behind, of an eggplant. He was a brisk walker, though, in spite of his size. I followed him through an iron gate and then down a mulch-covered track to a sidewalk. We entered a plywood tunnel along a construction zone and emerged to cross a side street into a coffee shop. There were low sofas and tables strewn with flyers and free local newspapers. We ordered at the counter.

"You don't strike me as a native Nashvillian," Van Brun said.

"I've lived in several places."

"Where's home?"

I ran off the list: Florida, Texas, et cetera.

"Young man, you can't have that many homes," he said. "A man has one home and one name."

"I have one name and I have had several homes," I said. My face was tingling.

We took seats. Van Brun straightened his back and set his chin on his left thumb, elbow on his knee. His teary gaze swept over the empty coffee shop. "You have the advantage over me," he said. "Tell me about your essay in précis form."

"I'm studying Andrew Johnson," I said. "Aspects of his life merit further attention."

"I am the author of *Partyless President*," Van Brun said.

"I know you are."

"Do you expect your work to supersede mine?"

"Of course not," I said. "Mine is narrower. I do not attempt the scope of a full biography."

Van Brun laughed. Here I experienced what I will call a "grayed out" state in which I was aware of his voice and perhaps responded to him with nods and assenting hums, but did not know what he was saying. This lasted, I think, not more than sixty seconds, until someone laughed sharply. It was the girl who had made our coffee, who was talking on a telephone.

"The well is dry," Van Brun said. "We've mined that vein clean. The *soil is spent.* Everything worth saying about Andrew Johnson was said some time ago—somewhat before my own time, I'm afraid."

"New materials may come to light," I said.

He harrumphed. "Have you found something?"

I was quiet. I let him guess.

"Yes. Well, things turn up in attics," he said. "One can sit waiting a hell of a long time for a pleasant surprise." He blew across his coffee. "What's your age?"

I told him.

"Heavens," he said.

"Is it unusual to be twenty-eight?"

"No, not unusual. It is young, though. Why don't you choose a different field?"

"I'm interested in Johnson."

"I don't care what you're *interested* in. There's no *future* in it. And I think if you made a fuller or perhaps keener study of the question, you would see that Andrew Johnson is a very sad specialization for a young man with years of potentially useful labor ahead of him. What makes you think new materials will surface anytime soon?"

"I have reason to believe some important Johnson papers were hidden by the president's family soon after his death," I said.

Van Brun's gaze softened. "I doubt that," he said in a low voice.

I asked him if he knew the name Winfield S. Lewis.

"Lewis," he repeated. His hand twitched with impatience. "He wrote a thing—an early, celebratory biography of Johnson. It exaggerates Johnson's heroism during the siege of Nashville, and there's also, if I remember correctly, a lengthy and lyrical paean to the Alaska Territory."

"Correct," I said. "The work itself has no historical value. What's interesting is Lewis's correspondence."

"Are you affiliated with any institution besides Triple-A?" Van Brun asked.

"Not even Triple-A, unfortunately."

"What have you got?"

"It's the scrapbooks," I said. "As you know, Johnson was a great preserver of clippings and notes."

"I made use of the scrapbooks in my biography," Van Brun said.

"Right. The ones in the state archives."

"Yes."

"There is another one," I said. "You missed one."

"What makes you think that?"

Though I had promised myself not to tell the lead at any cost, Van Brun's blustering was too much for me, and I let it spill. "I know it because I discovered a letter to Lewis from Johnson's daughter, Martha Patterson, in which she writes that she will not destroy a certain purple-bound scrapbook containing potentially compromising mementos from the earliest days of the Johnson presidency, as Lewis has urged, but will take care that the book is preserved in the family and kept from persons who might have an interest in its misuse!"

As I caught my breath, Van Brun shifted uncomfortably on the greasy sofa. He looked towards the ceiling and sniffed.

"Of course, by *misuse*," I went on, "what Mrs. Patterson meant was *any use that would damage Andrew Johnson's reputation*. She would spare no effort to protect her father's name. She believed him to have been the great-est American since Washington."

Van Brun chortled. He then fell quiet and looked at me pityingly. "I'm afraid you're making too much of something very small," he said. "I knew Mrs. Patterson's granddaughter, you know. Edna Johnson Patterson Jones. The poor thing. She was the last of the Johnson heirs to claim him. Viewed herself as local nobility, around Greeneville. Childless, too. I expect she's dead by now. If Mrs. Jones had had this scrapbook, she'd have presented it to me with a bow on top."

"Maybe she would have," I said. "If she'd had it."

"If she didn't have it, no one did. It's lost, or it never existed."

"Martha Patterson entrusted it to her nephew," I said. "She didn't want it among her papers when she died. She didn't want someone like *you* to find it, Dr. Van Brun."

"That's absurd," I said. "What sort of 'compromising mementos'?"

"You'll find out when I publish," I said.

My defiant tone seemed to please him. "Though implausible, this is all sort of intriguing," he said. "How can an entire profession have missed this letter?"

"It's at the New York City Public Library," I said.

"That doesn't make sense. Even there, out of the way, some Johnsonist would have noticed a letter from Martha Patterson."

"The box is mislabeled," I said. "She's listed as Martha Johnson *Peterson*."

"*Peterson?* Delightful!" He patted the tops of his legs.

"If true, you've done some fine research. Luck plus dili-
gence, that is the key. You may have a talent. Still, you're
visibly green."

He squirmed, huffing, and tugged at the waistline of
his trousers.

He went on. "Let me explain what I'm saying to you,
young man, from a position of some experience. *No one
cares* about Andrew Johnson. Years ago, I mean when I
was your age, everyone was interested because of the
civil rights connection, you see? We had Lyndon in the
White House, this big crude pottymouth, Great Society
and so on, and you could write a book about Andrew, who
was crude and *short-statured,* and had unwillingly
presided over the *first* wave of American civil rights legislation, and who had also like Lyndon succeeded a
beloved murdered president, and who most importantly
was also named Johnson, you see—which lent an attractive creepiness to the story. But that was thirty years ago,
and that is not where we are now. You should choose
something hot and of the moment. Find some founding
father and prove he was part Negro."

"That could be difficult," I said.

"It *must* be difficult, or someone would already have
done it, don't you see? That, there, is the secret to becoming necessary in any field of endeavor. You find a nearly
impossible task, and you do it, and then you are needed."

He popped his neck and asked me if I wanted a sandwich. I did but said no. He called to the girl at the
counter that he wanted a chicken salad sandwich "minus
bread."

I mentioned by way of conversation that I had become acquainted with a member of the legislature.

"Which one?"

"The Tennessee General Assembly."

"No, I mean which *member?*"

"Ronnie Runnels."

"Don't know him," Van Brun said. "Most of our legislators are terrific bores, I'm sorry to say. Many were bullied as children. I've met a number of them personally."

"How do you happen to meet them?"

"I go to lots of gala balls," he said. "Most of what I know, however, I have learned from studying the newspapers. There is no substitute for reading the news closely every day."

The girl brought a plastic bowl of chicken salad. Van Brun dug in with a spoon.

"Mr. Runnels represents the Sixth House District in Upper East Tennessee," I said. "He's from the Pantherville community."

"I don't know the place, but it sounds like some typical damp spot in the roadway like they have up there in the hills. Those hill people. Of course, Johnson was an East Tennessean. You know that, if you've written a paper on him. He hailed from Greeneville. Not originally, though."

Van Brun proceeded to recite to me many facts about Johnson which are well known to anyone who has read the *World Book Encyclopedia* entry on the seventeenth president of the United States. His voice crowded the long and narrow coffee shop, filling it up like a warm cloud. The coffee girl actually turned down her radio to listen. The voice was large and resounding, and Van Brun took an embarrassing pleasure in pronouncing words. Every diphthong received its due.

For nearly a minute he stared at a spot near my head while he spoke. He raised one hand suddenly, then smiled and narrowed his eyes. Theatrics such as these have their place in the lecture hall, with a few hundred undergraduates in attendance. He spilled some of the contents of his spoon onto the front of his shirt, and at last he had to get up and find a napkin. Now I was bored.

Up at the bar, Van Brun bantered loudly with the coffee girl. By an act of directed will I ignored them. He returned with a chocolate chip cookie seven inches across, enveloped in tissue. "This is for you," he said. "If I eat it I'll go into sugar coma. I feel rather badly about our misunderstanding and would like to make amends through the gift of this delicious baked good."

Though reluctant, I accepted the cookie.

"How do you happen to know the distinguished gentleman from Pantherville?" Van Brun said.

"I rode here with him this morning."

"All the way from upstate, you mean?"

"Yes."

"I hope he was interesting company," Van Brun said. "That's a long drive, as I recall." He gazed at me quietly for a moment, and then he said in a deeper voice, "I must away," and he left.

10

N ow I had some hours to kill. Dweena was not
due to pick me up until two, and there was no way
to contact her.

I walked up and down Twenty-third Street, then
crossed West End Avenue. On a side street a man asked
me to hold his knapsack while he went inside a storefront
to donate plasma. I asked him why he didn't hold the
knapsack himself, and he said he expected to fall asleep
while having his blood drawn.

I didn't want to hold or even touch this man's knapsack. To simplify the matter, I lied that I was in a rush to
keep an appointment with my dentist.

"If you're in such a rush, why are you staring in that
window looking at wigs for so long?"

"They caught my eye," I answered quickly. In fact I
had not been looking at the wigs but at the lonely-
seeming plaster heads on which they were displayed.

"See here," I said. "I'm not holding your bag, and I won't be drawn into an argument on the subject."

"You're just like everybody else," he said.

"Of course I am. Why aren't you?"

That gave him something to think about.

I came across a secondhand bookshop where I paid twelve dollars for a copy of the *Webster's New International Dictionary*, unabridged, second edition. It fit nicely in my zipper bag after I removed and ate the last sandwich. Then I hiked back to the bench at the edge of the Vanderbilt campus where I had agreed to meet Dweena. It was an arduous walk with the sixteen-pound dictionary at the end of my arm. I know the exact weight because I later weighed it using a bathroom scale.

Dweena Price was late. I read the Merriam-Webster "Introduction on Usage." I had read it once before, in the tenth grade, when I put in a stint as library assistant to Mrs. Nita Long at the Jim Clarke Middle School in Beaumont, Texas. One day in the library smoke came out of the ceiling, and Mrs. Long screamed.

Three o'clock passed, then four, then six. I began to recognize pedestrians who had passed me hours earlier. They were returning now, their business seen to. Perhaps some of them recognized me as well, the tweed-jacketed man with an oversized reference work on his lap.

It was close to seven o'clock when the white Wagoneer rolled to a stop at the curb. I got in and shut the door. "Where have you been?" I said. Before Dweena could answer I went on: "We agreed on two o'clock, and

I have been sitting here for four hours like a panhandler. I'm stiff from sitting."

"I was—"

"Of course I wondered if you'd been in an accident," I said. "I thought of calling the police, but to do that I would have had to leave the bench, and then what if you showed up while I was away? This whole day has been a disaster."

She pulled back into traffic and we rode. She didn't speak.

"So where were you?" I said.

"I got stuck in an income tax protest," she said.

"In a what?"

"There was a demonstration downtown, and they stopped traffic. The protesters blocked the streets, so we had to leave the Wagoneer to get Ronnie to the capitol in time for the vote. Then my Wagoneer got towed."

"It got towed? Where is Ronnie now?"

"On a sofa eating caramel corn, I imagine. Meanwhile I had to take a cab to the car pound," she said.

"Oh."

"The antitax people were blowing their car horns till the batteries ran down, to jam up the roads so the protax legislators would miss the vote. There was a guy coaching them on the radio—this conservative talk-show guy."

"Is Ronnie in favor of the income tax?"

"No. He's a no-tax vote. And there he was on his crutches in a mob. Finally we convinced some people who he was, and this guy in a pilgrim suit carried him the rest of the way."

"In a pilgrim suit?"

"Yes. And his friend had on a turkey suit."

"Why?"

"I don't know," she said.

"I owe you an apology," I said.

She looked at me, and then at my dictionary. "I'm tired," she said.

"Let's eat. Are you hungry?"

"I want to get home. We've got four and a half hours of driving ahead of us."

"We've got to eat, though. I'll buy, if we can perhaps go someplace very moderately priced."

She squinted at me.

"Here's a place," I said. I pointed at a Mexican restaurant. She frowned, then hit her turn signal.

Inside, we were seated in a booth. The waiter said, "¿Dos cervezas?"

"Bring me one," Dweena said.

"¿Habla Español?" I asked her.

"I know what *cerveza* is," she said.

"Una cerveza, por favor," I said to the waiter. "Y una agua."

The waiter scowled at me. "¿Una agua?"

"Si."

"¿Y una cerveza?"

"Si, si. Gracias."

He left.

"My day was a complete waste," I said. "I wish I had been stuck in the demonstration instead."

"Did you get your thing done with your editor man?"

"No. It was a humiliating waste of time," I said.

Dweena bit a corner off a large chip with salsa on it. She looked at me.

"I've had a few hours to think about it," I said. "I let myself be suckered by hope."

"Hm," Dweena said.

"This editor I met with is like something out of a science fiction film," I said. "Professor Meat Blob."

A waitress came with two giant goblets of beer. I told her in English that we had only ordered one.

"Thank you," she said. "You order food now?"

I let it go. We ordered, and she left.

"Is Mr. Runnels staying in Nashville?" I asked.

"Yes. He's got somebody he stays with when they're in session."

I questioned her about the background of the tax controversy and Runnels's position on it.

"Why do you want to know?" she said.

"Because I'm curious, of course. It must have been a frantic time, trying to get him to the House chamber before the vote was over."

"Mainly he was worried about getting there before they shut down the grill at the legislative cafeteria," she said.

I sipped my beer. I had never much liked the stuff, but I was thirsty and the beer was cold, which I found helped to keep the flavor down. In general, cold things have less flavor than warm, and also less smell.

I asked her whether she'd had to pay a fine to get her Wagoneer back.

"Yes."

"Maybe Runnels can get that refunded," I said.

"Ronnie doesn't do things like that," she said.

"There would be nothing unethical in it. As I recall, the Tennessee constitution provides that no member of the General Assembly may be subject to arrest on his way to a meeting of the legislature."

"I don't mean Ronnie's ethical," she said. "He just doesn't do things."

"Well, he's busy."

"No. That's not what I mean."

"Are you and he good friends?"

"We grew up together," she said. "But Ronnie is sort of Dwayne's case. Dwayne looks after him."

I remembered Dwayne, the postmaster.

"Dwayne looks after Boo, too," she said. "Dwayne likes looking after people."

"Why doesn't Boo work?" I asked.

She said he drew some disability money, and he made some from his dogs. He owned his place outright, having inherited it at his father's death. "He's lucky he didn't own it when he was convicted," she said. "They could have taken it from him."

I couldn't picture Boo as a felon, and I said so. She told me about the day he was arrested. The police showed up with body armor and a helicopter. They pulled him out of the bathtub.

"It was my husband that turned him in," she said.

"Oh," I said. "I didn't know you were—" Then I stopped, confused.

"I were," she said. "But I no longer are."

She raised her goblet with both hands and took a long drink.

The food came on plates that were too hot to touch. The waiter wore silver oven mitts. We fed. Dweena ate a taco and some Spanish rice, and I ate an enchilada, a chile relleno, a burrito, and Dweena's second taco. I ordered another of the large beers.

"I'm going to need a cup of coffee for the drive home," Dweena said.

"You won't want to drink the coffee here," I said. "I've got coffee left in my thermos."

"That coffee of yours is not so good," she said.

"Sure it is," I said. "Try the restaurant coffee if you want, though."

She turned and waved for the waiter.

I had been studying her somewhat. Her manner was quiet and reserved, but when she did speak it was with a striking frankness. Sometimes shy people, *because of their shyness,* never develop the highly complex verbal skill known as Talking Without Saying Anything. It is a skill that can be mastered only through practice, and you cannot practice it alone in your room. It has to be practiced in a group, with jaw in motion. There are professionals who can stand talking at the front of a room for thirty minutes, and then answer questions for another fifteen, without saying a single meaningful word.

It is a useful skill, and one that Dweena Price did not have. The only way she knew to stop herself saying what she meant was to keep quiet.

"Do you have any hobbies?" I asked her.

"I don't think so," she said.

"What do you do when you're not delivering mail?"

She looked at the plates and the basket with a few crumbs of chips left in the bottom. She shrugged.

"Do you subscribe to any magazines?" I asked.

"No."

"Do you read much?"

"I read books," she said.

"What authors? What have you read recently?"

She named a half-dozen titles.

"I don't know any of those," I said. "What are they, novels?"

"Yes."

I nodded. "Novels aren't my thing, though I have read *McTeague* by Frank Norris," I said. "Have you read that?"

"No."

Her coffee came. The waiter cleared the table, and when he started to take her beer goblet, I put my hand on it. She'd only drunk less than half of it. "You don't mind, do you?" I said.

"Why should I mind?"

"You might think it's a little forward of me to drink from your glass," I said.

"I didn't, until you said that," she said.

I described Van Brun to her. I told her about the meeting with him. It was a disappointment. The dejectedness, coming out of that meeting, was proportional to my euphoria going in.

She asked me where my family was.

"Mother's in California," I said. "With a husband. She's up in double digits now, on marriagings."

"Marriagings?"

My lips felt a little numb. I waved my hand in a dismissive gesture.

"Where are your friends?" she said.

"My good friend Terence is in Galena, Ohio," I said. "*Easy there,* old fellow."

"What about the friend you had the reading club with?"

"Shirley Walls. Shirley's in Galena, too. She works for the Water Department."

"Was she your girlfriend?"

"No, I don't think so. We ate together twice a week for four years, but she wasn't my girlfriend. It was mainly all about reading and commentary."

Dweena sipped some coffee. We sat quietly a moment and then she straightened up suddenly and pulled the rubber band out of her hair.

"She did propose to me," I said.

"Why didn't you marry her?"

"It was abrupt," I said. "Not expected."

"What did you tell her?"

"I said, 'Get up, Shirley.'"

"'Get up, Shirley'?"

"That's what I told her."

"You were in bed when she proposed?"

"No, no. I was in a chair. She had gotten down on her knee."

I could feel myself swaying a little in the booth seat. There was a bright serape tacked to the wall, and I looked at it for something to look at. The fabric was frosted with dust. I looked at Dweena's hand, on the table. The nails were even, with smooth cuticles. I glanced up and saw that she was watching me look at her hand, and I grabbed the ticket and excused myself to go to the register and pay.

Outside, I suggested that we take a walk across West End to see Centennial Park.

"We've got a long drive ahead," she said.

But she agreed. We walked up the sidewalk a bit, then ran to get to the crosswalk before the light changed. I tripped at the curb and sprawled on the pavement.

"Man down!" someone yelled.

I quickly got back to my feet and we crossed. There was something special I wanted to see before we left: the Nashville Parthenon.

The Parthenon of Nashville was built for the Centennial Exhibition of 1900. It is a one-hundred-percent scale replica of the original Parthenon in Athens, Greece, as imagined in its pre-ruined state. The only other difference is that the Nashville Parthenon is constructed of a brown-gravel aggregate concrete, whereas the Greek one is marble.

I had studied brochures, and I recited a few facts to Dweena as we crossed the park. "The reproduction of the Parthenon symbolized the effort of a provincial city to link itself with the most venerated traditions of world civilization and democracy," I said.

"What?"

"THE GLORY THAT WAS GREECE," I said. I caused my voice to resound, which made Dweena stop walking and look at me.

"Do that again," she said.

"I AM NOT A CROOK," I said.

"How do you do that?"

"My mother taught voice," I said. "I simply dilate my throat and project from the diaphragm."

Then we were there. The brown Nashville Parthenon was lit up with floodlights from the ground. Its columns bulged. "It's a marvel," I said. I was moved, and I couldn't find words to say how the thing made me feel.

"It's big," Dweena said. "And it's brown."

We climbed the tall steps at the side and found two monumental bronze doors, which were locked. We climbed back down in front and found the ground-level entrance, where tickets were sold. It was almost closing time but the clerk let us go in. "You won't have long," she said.

We passed the gift shop and took some stairs up to the main gallery or sanctuary. It was a huge hall lined on all four sides with two stories of columns. The coffered ceiling was far off and dark. At the end of this room, standing forty feet high and staring ardently into the emptiness over our heads, was the gold-draped figure of Athena, the Goddess of Wisdom.

"Wow," Dweena said.

The statue stood on a square pedestal with figures of Greek men and women in relief. Athena held a spear and a heavy shield, and in her outstretched right palm a small winged person waited, offering garlands. The god-dess's breasts were covered in a scaly armor, and her hel-met had five prongs. Her ivory arms were bare.

At her sternum a small face emerged, mouth open in a red scream. That was strange. But the two features that were most striking of all were her immense and shapely sandal-clad feet. The toes met me right at eye level. Her big toe was the size of my head.

"Those are some big feet," Dweena said.

"They're nicely proportioned, though," I said.

"I guess so. The toe knuckles are kind of high."

"The Greek foot isn't a naturalistic foot," I said. "It's conventionalized."

"It's a foot," Dweena said.

"I would add that the same Greeks who solved this problem of rendering the human foot in art were also well equipped to solve another and more important problem, namely government by the people."

"I don't follow you," she said.

"The Greeks invented citizenship," I said, "which is an idealization of the human individual, politically. And they invented this ideal foot, which appears noble and beautiful in stone. Unlike real feet, which are not."

"I'd have to disagree with you there," Dweena said. "Feet are okay if you take care of them."

"But some people don't," I said. I felt a sick twinge.

"Well I do, and you should," she said.

She had been studying some horses on the front of the pedestal, and now she turned around and looked at me. Her dark hair swung when she turned her head.

From the rear of the hall someone whistled. "We'll be closing," the man said. A door clicked, and the click echoed.

"You have a healthy attitude towards feet," I said.

Dweena's brown eyes grew slightly rounder, and then she smiled.

"Do you smell metal?" I said.

"I smell *cerveza*," she said.

"No, really," I said. "I think I'm about to have an episode."

"What are you talking about?"

"I'll keep standing up," I said. "Just pull my sleeve and maybe I'll be able to walk."

She came close and took hold of my arm.

All I remember then is the sensation of my mouth continuing to move. Apparently I went on talking for a while. Then I was out like a porch light.

When I came to, it was very dark, and I was strapped in the passenger seat of the Wagoneer. I looked over at Dweena and saw her profile, lit faintly again in the light from the dashboard gauges.

11

I WAS DISCOURAGED BY THE Van Brun episode, and the next day I didn't do anything but read and eat cereal. I avoided Dweena. I'm not an especially prideful person, but I know when I've made a fool of myself. On Wednesday morning I was sleeping late again when Boo woke me up knocking on the front door. Mother had called with "urgent news."

"Is she leaving Zimmer?"

"How do I know?" Boo said.

I hurried down with him to use the phone. It turned out Mother's news was that she had been a contestant on a television game show called *This Changes Everything*. Though she was not permitted contractually to tell me the result, she did want me to know when and on what network the program would be broadcast. I wrote the information down.

Boo gave me a large plastic cup of Mountain Dew on ice. "You look like Puffy Man," he said.

I asked him if he had some coffee.

"What you've got right there is better than coffee," he said.

I drank some Mountain Dew, and it perked me up some. "I've got to get to work, Boo," I said.

"Okay," Boo said.

I needed to get to Greeneville. The Duster was parked on a red-clay lot at Mark's Repair, and Mark wanted four hundred dollars to install a rebuilt water pump. My savings of two hundred twenty dollars had shrunk to fifty-nine. I asked Boo if he could drive me into Greeneville.

We were at the kitchen table, and he had pushed his chair back and was bent forward rubbing waterproofing cream into his boots. He sat up and gave me a look. "Greeneville is a thirty-minute drive," he said.

We had not discussed his migraine ruse or the reason for it. I gathered, though, that he knew it had been explained to me. I said, "Suppose I drive the truck, and you ride?"

"It isn't who drives that matters," he said. He winked without smiling.

When the boots were ready he put them on and we went behind his house to the dog runs. Brownie lived in the house, but each of the working dogs had its own outdoor chain-link pen with a roof over part of it. There were nine of them. Boo stared hard at the dogs, as though he were reading their hides.

"But you may borrow my truck and go without me," he said.

He drew me a complicated map on a paper towel with

a black felt-tip pen, emphasizing that it was not to scale. "Watch for the baby mule and then take your next right. That will be Bill Ford Road," he said.

"What if the baby mule isn't there?"

"Turn anyway."

"How will I know it?"

"Do you know what a mule looks like? It has a big head, and this particular mule is black. It will be standing beside its mother in a little muddy barn lot."

"Okay. Two mules."

"No, John. One mule, and its mother."

I watched carefully and never did see the mare or her mule baby. Eventually I got directions from a man on an adult-sized tricycle who was gathering aluminum from the roadside. I made it into town.

The city of Greeneville is the seat of Greene County, named for General Nathan Greene of the Revolutionary War. At the time of Andrew Johnson's arrival, in 1826, the town possessed a courthouse and two private academies. People whose only knowledge of the story is derived from the 1942 MGM film *Tennessee Johnson* will have the mistaken impression that the future president showed up in Greeneville wearing an iron cuff on his leg and trailing a length of chain. In fact this is a bit of Hollywood license-taking. While it is true that Johnson had broken a legally binding apprenticeship and had a bounty on his head, what tailor holds his boy in a leg iron? Who would patronize that tailor?

Van Heflin portrayed Andrew Johnson in the biopic. Another inaccuracy promulgated by the film is that

Johnson served a term as county sheriff. He never did, though he might have been an effective one. In 1861, after declaring on the Senate floor his wish to see secessionists hung, he was confronted by a mob of angry Virginians and subdued them with his pistol.

I found the Greeneville courthouse. I was searching for any clue about the life of Johnson's grandson, Robert Stovall. Stovall was the heir to whom Johnson's daughter Martha had entrusted the compromising purple book, according to her letter. The courthouse had nothing on him: no birth or marriage certificate, no tax records—no reference to Robert Stovall of any kind. I did leave with ten bags of expired cheese snacks, which were given to me by a man who was servicing the vending machine.

I visited the Andrew Johnson National Historic Site. It is kept by the Park Service and includes Johnson's home and the famous one-room tailor shop. The latter had become a kind of shrine—a rough clapboard building with a brick museum enclosing it. Inside was the tall worktable atop which Johnson had sat cross-legged, sewing.

The house was a modest one, for an ex-president. It was built right up against the street in downtown Greeneville, with only a sidewalk between the front steps and the public road. This was the house where, soon after the war, Johnson's oldest son had died from a self-administered dose of laudanum. It was the house where Johnson chose not to write his memoirs—why?—but instead to run for office again, failing twice before he won back his former place in the Senate. He gave one final speech from the Senate floor, attacking President Grant, then died of a stroke in 1875.

The rooms were small, as was the furniture. It is difficult to keep in mind how tiny most of our forefathers were. Johnson himself was about the size of Boo, who drove with his truck seat slid all the way up to the steering wheel.

I asked the tour guide, a young female park ranger, what she knew about Robert Stovall.

"He was known as the reclusive one," she said. "The black sheep."

This made some sense. Whatever secrets the purple book held—campaign improprieties? excesses from Johnson's years as military governor?—would have to be kept from most of the family as well as from the historians. Martha Patterson might well have chosen Stovall *because* he was the black sheep. "Do you know where he lived when he died?" I asked.

"When he died he was dead, I guess." The guide laughed brightly at her joke, as did a class of fifth-graders who were along for the tour.

"I'm sorry," I said. "What I meant to ask was, do you know where he lived *just prior to* his death?"

"I do not," she said. "Why are you interested?"

"I'm just curious about anything Johnson-related," I said evasively.

The teacher who had brought her class observed, "Johnson is one of the presidents we don't hear much about."

"His story is not the most interesting," a boy said.

"I have to disagree," I said to the boy. "The trial in the

Senate of Andrew Johnson was one of the most dramatic and dangerous moments in our nation's history. *Harper's Weekly*, which was a magazine read by grown-ups, predicted that the president would call up the army before he relinquished his office. Senator Sumner wanted the president to be thrown in jail! There might easily have been a second civil war, only this time, it would have been not a war between the states, but a war between the branches of the government."

The boy gave me a hostile stare.

"You should be interested in Johnson because he is from your town," the teacher said.

"I'm from Spring Hill," the boy said.

"Then you should be interested in Polk," the tour guide said.

When the tour was over I walked down Main Street a little ways and stepped into a café I had passed driving in. It was mid-afternoon, and the place was almost empty. A man took my order of a glass of water, a patty melt, and a side of jo-jo fries. I asked him if he knew any Johnsons who lived in the area.

"Everybody knows somebody named Johnson," he said.

"Of course. I mean descendants of President Andrew Johnson. I thought that would be clear since we are just a few steps up the street from the National Historic Site." I mentioned that I was recently in from New York and working on some Johnson-related research.

"Today must be New York City day," the man said. "This lady here is from a New York TV news show."

He moved his head to indicate the only other person

in the café, a woman in a beige skirt and blouse perched on a chrome stool at the counter. She gave me a New York–style warning glance, then flicked her narrow eyebrows and turned away.

The warning glance was not the only giveaway. In fact, her New Yorker–hood showed in every aspect of her carriage and costume. One saw it even in her shoes, the shape of which had little to do with the form of any human appendage.

I eavesdropped on her exchange with the proprietor. She had been served a salad and she asked for a cruet of olive oil. He said that he had no olive oil, and she said she would take any sort of expeller-pressed salad oil as a substitute. He said he didn't know what "expeller-pressed salad oil" was and she said, "For example, any medium-quality or better canola oil." He said he didn't have any canola oil and she asked him was he sure of that, and he said no, he wasn't sure. Then after a pause she asked for some mayonnaise in a dish. She pronounced "mayonnaise" with three syllables, laying stress on the third. "That I can give you" the man said.

He brought my patty melt. The bread was nearly translucent with grease. It was quite tasty. The woman had gone to the ladies' room, and when she returned she stopped by my table. "You're from the city?" she said.

I wiped my hands and slid out of the booth seat to stand, as I was taught to do when meeting someone, male or female.

She backed several steps away from me as though I had threatened her. "Take it easy," she said.

Already it had begun. I sat down and invited her to do the same.

"I don't think so," she said.

"My name is John Tolley," I said. "I'm here doing historical research on Andrew Johnson."

"Yes, he came from here," she said. "A former president, correct?"

"That's right. He was president after the Civil War."

"That's what I just said, right?" She sniffed. "I'm also here on research."

"What are you researching?"

"We had a tip concerning a rash of four-handed babies in the area. I just flew in. Incidentally, I wouldn't be drinking that water. It's tap." She nodded at my glass.

She was a thin woman. Her hair was bolt straight with the dull sheen of bare aluminum. Her hands were thin and the nails were perfectly manicured. She had an unusually long nose—her most striking feature, easily. It was thin like a shoulder blade and slightly bent to one side. She sorted through her small purse and gave me a business card with her name, Danielle McBain, and the name of the program she worked for, *Point Blank*, a cable news show which I had seen a few times. I had not seen Ms. McBain on the show. She mentioned that she worked "behind camera," in production, piecing the story together ahead of time. A majority of the work was done this way, she explained. Next to arrive was the camera crew, followed finally by the celebrity "investigative *reporton*," who flies in for "stand-ups," then returns to the city to record his voice-overs.

That sounded like a poor arrangement, I said. If she

did most of the work ahead of time, it would make better sense for her to also do the reporting on television.

"It would sort of make sense, wouldn't it?" she said. "But that's not the way it operates, Mr. Tolley. We have a way of doing things, and what you describe is not it."

"I see."

"The producers do the footwork, and the *reportons* do the stand-ups. The reporton may imply that he has done the footwork. He'll say, '*Point Blank* has learned this or that.' When you hear him say that '*Point Blank* has learned this,' what you should understand is, 'My producer has learned this, and I am now sharing the credit for it.'"

"Why don't you become a reporton, so you can do the footwork and the reporting as well?" I said.

"I will never work in front of the camera for the obvious reason," she said.

"What obvious reason?" I asked.

She glared at me and sat down. "Don't be mean," she said.

I considered. "I don't know what you're talking about," I said.

"I'm talking about my enormous honker, obviously. My 'ventral fin,' as a boyfriend used to call it. It's cruel of you to make me say that. Thanks for nothing."

Six months previously, this rhetorical parry of hers would have left me licking my wounds. I understood it now as the New Yorker's way. It was only mock anger—a display of vigilance, the content of which could be paraphrased in the words, *I am paying attention to you.*

"I don't see your nose as a problem," I said, "but if you think so, why don't you have surgery on it?"

She didn't react right away. New Yorkers often don't, having heard every type of comment before. After a few seconds, slowly, she swayed back in her seat and allowed her mouth to drop open. She rolled her eyes towards the ceiling, which was clad in pressed tin and was quite high—perhaps fifteen feet.

"Are you telling me to have rhinoplasty?" Ms. McBain asked.

"If that's the only thing between you and becoming a reporter, why not?"

"That is an offensive opinion," she said. "You offend me."

"How do I offend you? I'd be glad to have you on television as you are. You're the one who said you can never go on television."

"No, I never said that! A producer told me that. A successful producer named Jerry Hedberg, maybe you've heard of him, told me I could never go in front of the camera with this nose because it would not be accepted by the American public."

"If anyone's offensive it's that producer," I said.

"He is not offensive! He's a very dear friend who had the courage and consideration to be straight with me about the realities of the television news business."

"Anyway if you're looking straight at the camera no one would particularly notice your nose. You wouldn't give the news in profile, would you?"

She shook her head quickly and rose from her seat. "I can't have this energy-sapping conversation," she said.

She pointed two fingers at the man who had served us, who was now scraping the grill with a tool that looked like a hoe, except it had a shorter handle. "Have you been paid?" she asked him.

He turned and looked at her. "What are you talking about?" he said.

"I'm asking whether you were paid yet for the food. The salad."

"Are you asking me whether *you* have paid?"

"Never mind," she said. "I'll pay, though I didn't eat very much." She laid a bill on the counter and waited there while the man took the bill and walked with it to the other end of the counter, where the register was, under a sign saying "Pay Here." She tapped her shoe. He brought her change, and she left.

I said a few words to him concerning the scene that had taken place. "I'm not originally from New York, but I lived there for six months. I can tell you that what you just saw is nothing unusual. New Yorkers are different. It's because of the way they live. They're accustomed to conditions of extreme physical closeness, where they're forever bouncing off each other. Also, their city is in some respects the capital of the world, and they feel this. Their opinion is that in order to live as they do, they have to stay in continual training, like athletes. It's an exertion they feel at all times, and they carry it with them wherever they go. Thus, Ms. McBain—though she has come to Tennessee, she has brought New York with her in the form of a clear shell which she cannot step outside of. It's a bubble. The business with the mayonnaise is typical."

He leaned against his short-handled hoe, the blade in a trough at the foot of the grill. "Thanks for the explanation," he said.

"You're welcome. Returning to the other subject, do you or don't you know any descendants of Andrew Johnson?"

"I don't."

"Okay. Have a nice day," I said. "I'm leaving my payment plus tip here on the table."

"Come back soon," he said.

12

I BOUGHT MYSELF A COPY of the weekly Greeneville paper, where I read about the protest demonstration that had temporarily stranded Representative Runnels and Dweena in downtown Nashville. Dweena had mentioned a talk-radio host who made use of his show to marshal the protesters; evidently he'd been in league with an antitax legislator who fed him up-to-the-minute e-mail dispatches from the House floor. His listeners had all but shut down the capital by stalling their cars in the streets. At the governor's office, someone smashed a window. The income tax proposal was thoroughly dead.

One could see that these Tennesseans had strong opinions on how they ought to be taxed. Their sales tax was the highest in the country, but they preferred it this way. They had rather pay tax on the consumption and not on the production. The sales tax on groceries was 9 percent, and that added up quickly, but the point was that a person could control the tax he paid by controlling the amount of groceries he consumed.

Of course, as one Greenevillian pointed out in a letter to the editor, a third of Tennessee families were classified by the federal government as "working poor," with many of these headed by single parents; to tax the working mother at the rate of 9 percent on each loaf of bread or pound of chuck she brought home might seem a little hard. But far more of these Tennessee working mothers suffered from obesity-related threats to their health than from starvation, he argued. "Starvation as a social phenomenon was virtually eliminated from the state of Tennessee in the twentieth century." If the state honestly wanted to help its single mothers and their children as well, he wrote, it would *raise* the tax on food, causing these people to *eat less* and feel better, too. "Adult men are more liable to burn calories through yard work and similar activities," he concluded.

In funding of its public schools, the state ranked forty-ninth. A small article at the back of the first section noted that the legislature had addressed this matter by proposing a state lottery, with the proceeds reserved entirely for education. There was an obstacle: the Tennessee constitution forbade it. Therefore a referendum would be held on whether to change the constitution.

I drove back to Boo's, parked the truck in his driveway, and hiked up the knob to the log house. My door was unlocked, as always. I hadn't been given a key. In the front room, in the middle of the floor, I found an empty wire cage standing open and a note on top that said,

"John I have left a Coon, please don't let her go. Come to supper."

I was trying to make some sense of this when I glanced up at the daybed and had a start. A big-bellied raccoon was watching me from the vinyl plaid mattress. It rose up on its rear legs and opened its mouth.

I ran down the hill. An orange Chevrolet pickup and a black coupe were parked in front of the little barn that was across from Boo's house, so I went that way, calling for Boo. Behind the barn I came upon Boo and two other men. They were emptying some large gray canvas bags onto the grass.

All three of them looked up at me. A tall man with blond hair said, "Who the hell is that guy?"

"That's John and he lives here," Boo said. He beckoned me over, but the blond man grabbed Boo's arm. Boo twisted away from him. "No touch!" Boo said.

The third man, whom I recognized, came towards me smiling. It was Dwayne Loupe, the postmaster. "Hello, sir," he said. He stopped right in front of me as though to block my view of the pile of yellow bundles that they had emptied onto the ground. He offered his hand, and we shook.

"I didn't mean to interrupt," I said. "There's a coon in my house."

The blond man stepped up beside Loupe. His skin was pink, and he had the looks of a catalog model. He wore a tie. His white shirt was paper-smooth. "You live here?" he said to me.

"John rents the old house," Loupe said.

"*Oh*," the blond man said. "You're *renting*. I thought maybe we had a new member of the family."

Loupe gave him a long, deadpan look.

The blond man sniffed and used a handkerchief to wipe his face. "I've got to run," he said. He left in the black car as Loupe led me by my arm towards Boo's house.

"Are you coming to supper?" Boo said.

"I don't know," I said. "I've never had raccoon."

"Never had raccoon? Son, where are you from?" Loupe asked.

"Florida, Texas, Scotland, and Ohio," I said.

He narrowed his eyes. "Everywhere but here," he said.

"When he leaves he'll be from here," Boo said.

"Well, Boo," the postmaster said, "are you going to show him how we cook a big pot of greasy raccoon goulash?"

"I didn't think we'd eat coon tonight," Boo said.

"What about the one in the cage?" I said.

"I'm not cooking Betty," Boo said.

"Betty?"

"Old Betty," Loupe said.

Then I remembered that she wasn't in her cage. I told Boo.

"You didn't take the towel off, did you?" Boo said.

"There wasn't any towel," I said.

"Are you sure?"

"There was an open cage with a note on top and a raccoon on my mattress with its jaws open," I said.

We had reached Boo's front yard. Boo said quietly, "Well now." He took the tin from his pocket and got a dip of tobacco. He handed the tin to Dwayne Loupe, who also took a pinch. Loupe's hand was thick, and his fingernails were shaped like little car hoods. The pinch he took was necessarily large: if he'd wanted a small one, he would have had to ask for help. He passed the tin to me, and I took a pinch and returned it to Boo. Boo looked up at the sky.

I put my pinch of tobacco in place behind my lip. "Do you ever eat raccoons?" I asked.

"Not me," Boo said. "They're not to my taste."

"What is the purpose of coon hunting, then?"

"It's a sport," he said.

"And don't the dogs kill the raccoon when they catch it?"

"They don't 'catch' it, John. They *tree* it."

"They *make it run up a tree,*" Loupe said.

"And then what?" I said.

"We go home," Boo said.

"That's the end of it? Raccoon in tree?"

"Game over," Boo said.

"Has Betty been treed?"

"Many times."

I asked him why Betty was in my house.

"The dogs can smell her up here," he said. "It's like anything else—if they smell her all day, they won't smell her tonight."

"Not everybody knows that," Loupe said. "It's kind of a trade secret."

"That's right," Boo said. "So keep it under your darn hat."

"Betty has a strong smell," I said.

"How would you describe her smell?" Loupe asked.

"Like wet cardboard," I said. I took a few steps to one side to spit.

"You couldn't smell her from across the woods, though," Boo said. "Any fool can smell a coon across his living room."

Loupe and I settled into chairs. Boo sat down backwards across the seat of a four-wheeler that was parked at the rear of the carport. Loupe said, "Did either of you boys ever get a smell stuck in your nose, and it wouldn't come out?"

"No," Boo said.

It had happened to me a few times.

"The worst smell I ever smelled was ant-killing granules," Loupe said.

"Not me," Boo said.

Loupe asked him what was worse.

"I don't want to go into it," Boo said.

"In Texas I saw a man catch his bathrobe on fire," I said. "He was trying to burn an ant pile out of his yard with a propane torch."

"That won't work," Boo said. "You've got to soak it with kerosene."

Loupe twisted to look at him.

"Well it's true," Boo said.

Boo displayed no sense of urgency about returning Betty the coon to her cage. This surprised me, but I chose not to reach for the sense of it, just as I chose not to wonder what it was that the men had been dumping from bags behind the barn. They'd looked like mail bags. But now was a time to "set awhile." Everyone spit. Boo used a plastic Mountain Dew bottle, and Loupe was near the edge of the concrete and could spit into the grass from his chair. I was across the table from Loupe and had to get up to spit, and I seemed to be spitting more than the others did, too. This was probably due to inexperience, although it was the second time and not the first that I had dipped tobacco. The first time ended with me vomiting, and I did not intend to vomit this time. I did, while rising to spit, get my foot tangled in the legs of the awkwardly lightweight plastic patio chair. Boo asked me if I was getting a head buzz.

"A little bit," I said.

Loupe asked, "Did you get to know my niece better on your trip?"

"I don't know your niece," I said.

"That's a hell of a comment, after you kept her out all day and half the night."

"You mean *Dweena*," I said. "I didn't know she was your niece. She must be named after you, then."

"She's named after my brother," Loupe said.

"Uncle Ed," Boo said.

"Edwina Louise Price," Loupe said. "My damn sure good enough niece."

"Is Price her maiden name?" I asked.

Loupe frowned at me. "Yes," he said.

"John had one of his trance states while looking at a barefoot statue," Boo said.

"It was a long day, Boo," I said.

"Are you at all conscious during those?" he asked.

"No."

"So you have no idea what you said or done during that time."

"I didn't do anything," I said.

"You done something," Boo said.

"Did he try to kiss her?" Loupe asked.

"I promised not to tell," Boo said.

"I didn't kiss anybody," I said.

"You better not have done any *more* than kiss her," Loupe said.

I can take a little teasing. I was quiet. Then I felt a twinge in my stomach, and I had to get up and spit out my tobacco in the yard. A hen shot over and pecked at it near my feet in the grass. It was a tall but skinny hen.

"Is this chicken full-grown?" I asked.

Boo nodded.

"She's kind of lean," I said.

"No she's not," Loupe said. "Look at those feathers. Look at her head. That's a healthy bird. What you see there is what an adult chicken is meant to look like."

"She doesn't have much meat, though."

"She's not a fryer, John," Loupe said. "Your modern fryer is an abnormally overmeated bird."

"Is this bird not modern?" I asked.

"What that is is a very special bird," Loupe said. "It's called a greenleg Panamanian."

This special bird was disappointed with my tobacco, though. She wandered away, pecking at the grass. I remembered the ten bags of expired cheese puffs in the cab of the truck, and I got a bag and tossed a cheese puff into the grass for her. A rooster that had been ignoring me up to now shot over and pecked at the cheese puff twice. He made a sound like water about to boil: *rrrrr*.

"He's looking out for his hen," Loupe said.

When the rooster had finished inspecting the cheese puff he backed away, and the hen came and ate it. I dropped some more cheese puffs to the ground. Their oily orange powder coating stuck to my fingertips.

Boo said, "What are you feeding those birds?"

I told him the story of the cheese puffs, and he went to the truck and brought back the remaining nine bags and spread them out on the patio table. He opened a bag for himself and handed a bag to Dwayne Loupe. Loupe studied it, then set it down unopened.

I asked Loupe when he expected Representative Runnels back from Nashville.

"He's back. The session is over," Loupe said.

Boo dropped his cheese puffs bag. "I've got to brush my teeth before I can enjoy these," he said. He went into the house.

"I'd love to hear him tell the story of the big tax vote," I said.

"The big story is the lottery vote," Loupe said. "Ronnie switched sides and caused it to pass by a margin of one."

"Is that right?" I repeated the story of the dramatic vote on the seventh article of impeachment in the Senate trial of President Johnson. The Republicans had counted and recounted the likely votes; but the conscience of Senator Edmund Ross wasn't subject to party discipline. His vote acquitted the president but ended the senator's career.

"This will end Ronnie's career," Loupe said, "but it wasn't because of his conscience. He got suckered."

"How?"

"Can you keep it to yourself?"

"Who would I tell? The only people I know here are you, Boo, and Dweena."

Loupe spit into the grass. "Here's what happened. Did you ever play basketball?"

"In grade school," I said.

"Did you ever know a boy who, you could call out his name and he'd throw you the ball, even though you were on the other team?"

"I knew of such a boy," I admitted.

"Well, this is what happened to Ronnie. Mike told him, 'Ronnie, remember to vote yes on the lottery bill,' and Ronnie did it."

"I never considered that sporting behavior," I said.

Loupe shrugged. "That's politics," he said. "The other man's weakness is your strength. Ronnie's weakness is that he's simple-minded."

"He can't be too simple. He got himself elected."

"Wrong. He got himself appointed by the county to fill a vacant seat. And they did it after being made to understand that Ronnie was strictly opposed to taxes, gambling, and all forms of sin."

"Who is Mike?"

"Mike Signet. He's the crook that used to hold the seat Ronnie has. He resigned and now he's an unregistered lobbyist for Data Branch Incorporated, breaking laws left and right."

"What is Data Branch Incorporated?"

"A bunch of Swedes."

"Doing what?"

"Never mind," Loupe said. "Hush hush."

The door had swung open, and Boo came back out to the carport. He got his cheese puffs from the table and settled onto the four-wheeler to eat them.

Loupe said, "Son, what size is your foot?"

"My foot?" I said.

"Yes, yours."

I told him.

"Wait right here," he said. He rose and walked off towards the orange truck parked by the barn.

Boo said, "Yep, Dweena told me all about what you said during your supposed blackout."

"Very funny, Boo. *Ha ha.*"

"I didn't think it was funny. Neither did she."

"Let me guess. Did I tell her, 'I love you'? Did I ask her to elope with me?"

"You told her she has a face like a monkey," Boo said.

"*No!*"

"A certain kind of monkey whose name I can't pronounce. But it has a long swinging nose, according to you."

Another wave of sickness hit me.

Loupe was back. He set down a pair of work boots in front of my chair. "Try those on," he said.

"Why?"

"To see if they fit," Loupe said.

I removed my wing tips and pulled the boots on.

"Walk around in them some," Loupe said.

I did it.

"I've been carrying those boots around for a year, looking for someone to give them to," Loupe said.

"They're too small for most men's feet," Boo said.

"They weren't too small for *your* feet," Loupe said.

"No, they're too large for me, but I have a small frame," Boo said. "You have a large frame, Dwayne."

"Good-bye," Loupe said. He spit his tobacco into the grass and went back to his truck.

"Did she seem very upset?" I asked Boo.

"She was none too flattered, John."

"What am I going to say to her now?"

"There's no telling."

Across the one-lane road, Loupe was sitting in his truck with his hand on the wheel. Another vehicle was coming up the road, and he had to let it pass before he could leave. It was Dweena in her white Wagoneer. She pulled into the driveway alongside Boo's truck, and Loupe drove away, and Boo got up and went to the door of his house.

"Boo! Don't leave me!" I said.

"I'll just be right in here, John." He went inside.

Dweena got out and headed across the yard towards the far end of the house, where her separate entrance was. "Hello, Dweena," I said.

She stopped. "Hello, John," she said. "Feeling better?"

"Yes, thanks." I had slept or pretended to sleep the

whole way home from Nashville, and we hadn't talked since that night. "No more seizures," I said. "It's a medical condition completely beyond my control."

She nodded. She was wearing her usual blue coveralls and black work boots, similar to the ones I had on, and her hair was in its rubber band.

"Your uncle just gave me some boots," I said.

"He's been trying to give them away for a year," she said.

"You look nice today," I said. "You have a pretty face."

Her neck turned red and she walked away, across the yard and around the corner of the house.

I went in the carport door and found Boo at his kitchen table, peeling potatoes. I sat down.

"How did it go?" he said.

"I need medical, possibly psychiatric help," I said.

"That gets expensive," Boo said.

"I know it. And I don't have the money."

"Try some potato therapy," he said. He handed me a potato and the peeler.

I took some swipes at the potato. "I want you to tell her it wasn't what it sounded like," I said. "It was just a crazy association I made in my head."

"Dweena's a nice-looking person," Boo said.

"Of course she is," I said. I took a breath and started peeling very fast.

"What's your hurry? Are you hungry?"

"No," I said. "I mean, yes." I nicked my finger, then slowed down to peel at a normal rate.

"She hasn't gotten out much since divorcing the

skunk," Boo said. "He was the one I went to prison because of. How do you like them apples?"

"I don't know what to say about it, Boo. Growing marijuana's illegal."

"I know that," he said, studying me.

"Why did he turn you in?"

"Did you ever hear of a person who vacuumed his way to the top?" Boo said.

"No."

"Rising by suction?"

"I don't follow you."

"He was trying to get in good with the sheriff," Boo said. "But the sheriff wound up losing the next election anyway, and so the skunk didn't get any good out of it. I know a thing or two about him that I could tell to the law, but that's not how I operate."

"It's good to focus on future plans," I said blandly.

"I'll say this," Boo said. "You've got to look out and be careful who you marry. Did you ever come close?"

"I'd have to say no," I said.

"Me neither. Not to say I never would. But in my position it's a tricky deal, since I own this house and land, twenty-six acres, and I draw my disability each month, plus Dweena's rent, plus your rent, now that you're here. Anytime a woman, you know, *approaches* me, I have to wonder, is she looking at me or is she looking at that house, that property, those dogs, and that monthly income? And I won't have a woman who smokes," Boo said.

"No."

"What kind would you see yourself marrying, John?"

"I don't see myself ever marrying. It would be cruel."

"If you did, though."

I thought about the question. "Someone feminine," I said.

"I'm that way, too."

"I don't mean submissive," I said. "She'd have to have a spine. But I wouldn't want a girl who carries a thick billfold around in her hip pocket."

Boo made a sour face.

"The old roles are not all bad," I said. "I do read magazines, and I'm aware that the ground rules have changed in recent years. There's no reason, today, why the woman has to be the wife and the man the husband. The man can be the wife. Or they can both be wives, both the man and the woman; or both of them can be husbands, for that matter, or the woman can be the husband and the man some other thing. When I say the words 'husband' and 'wife,' I am referring to the *roles*, with all the responsibilities appertaining thereto."

"Uh-huh. Keep going," Boo said.

"*My* choice, if I were to marry," I said, "would be for *me* to be the *husband*, and for the *woman* to be the *wife*. That's the way *I'd* like to have it, though I'm not saying it's natural law."

Boo was quiet for a time, and then he said, "I think I follow you, John. That's about the best thing I ever heard anybody say."

"Surely not," I said.

"No, it is. Most people around here don't talk like you. I could picture you on certain channels of television."

"The History Channel, maybe?"

"Maybe. Or something even more that way."

We peeled and sliced half a sack of potatoes, then Boo cooked them in a Pyrex dish with cheese and milk and we ate the whole thing. It was a good, satisfying meal. Afterwards we hiked up the knob to the log house. It was dark, and I carried a flashlight. Boo wore his strap-on forehead lamp. When we got to the log house we switched them both off. "Follow me quietly," Boo said. "I'm going to steer the coon using darkness."

I followed him into the house and shut the door. I heard him place the cage in a corner of the front room. He then switched on his forehead lamp, which he'd pivoted downward so that it lit a bright oval on the floor. I handed him the flashlight. He stepped into the kitchen, clicking his tongue.

Pretty soon, here came Betty from the kitchen doorway. I heard her scratching steps and faintly saw her transversely barred tail. Between the two oblongs of light, Boo had formed a movable wedge of darkness that the raccoon, with her predilection for not being seen, was doing her best to stay inside of. The wedge of darkness crossed the floor, and then I heard the cage creak lightly as Betty stepped inside. Boo shut the door with his foot.

"You can turn on the ceiling light now," Boo said.

I found the switch and there she was inside the cage, watching us without surprise from behind her black mask. It was a nice job of coon handling, and I told Boo so.

"Everyone's good at something," he said.

"I certainly hope so," I said.

13

WHO MIGHT KNOW WHAT had become of Robert Stovall? Though its perusal was now distasteful to me, I opened Van Brun's *Partyless President* and studied the brief acknowledgments page. He had offered his "profoundly heartfelt thanks" to Mrs. Edna Johnson Jones, "the President's great-granddaughter." This was the woman he had mentioned in our conversation. The copyright date of his book was 1969.

Even supposing that she was still alive and had not left the area, how many hundreds of Mrs. Joneses must there be in East Tennessee? There might even be thousands.

I borrowed Boo's truck and did searches at the Sullivan, Washington, Carter, and Unicoi County courthouses, where I came up with nothing. I questioned clerks, custodians, and even people waiting in line to renew their car tags. I got many quizzical looks. "People from here don't care a lot about Andrew Johnson," one man said.

I asked him where he was from.

"I'm from here," he said.

A sheriff's deputy who was standing by the metal detector and who had overheard this exchange told me there was a man in Bristol who owned an English china plate that Andrew Johnson had dined from while he was president. There was also some cutlery, a napkin, a soap dish and towel, and a bone from the goose that was served. The deputy didn't know the man's name, though.

I went back to Greeneville and spoke again to the guide at the National Historic Site, who was also the site's director, I learned. She was eager to help, but all that she knew was drawn either from the standard sources with which I was already familiar or from some notes that had been handed down in typescript by the Park Service staff, and which were incompletely documented. The notes claimed that Stovall, still a bachelor, had left Greeneville sometime during the 1890s and never come back.

"Who wrote the notes?" I asked her.

"A Johnson biographer, years ago—Van Bloom? Van Plum?"

I thanked her and left. Going back to Van Brun was out of the question. I had sooner choke on the Johnson goose bone.

I was climbing back into Boo's truck when it occurred to me I had forgotten to ask the most obvious question. I went back inside the brick building that housed the tailor shop and the little museum. "There was a great-granddaughter of Johnson's, Mrs. Edna Johnson Jones," I said. "Do you know anything about her?"

"I may," she said. She walked across the museum to a case that held some curled-up strips of leather. *"A pair of slippers given to Andrew Johnson by the King of the Sandwich Islands,"* she read. *"Donated by Mrs. Edna Johnson Jarvis."*

"Jarvis? That could be her name from a second husband!"

"Or a third!"

"When were the slippers given to the museum?"

"I don't know," the director said. "They've been here longer than I have, and I'd like to give them back."

She checked her files but could find no further record of the slippers' donor. Still, this name gave me something to work with. Phoning every Jarvis in Upper East Tennessee was a task I might be able to manage. I drove back to Boo's and told him I needed to borrow his phone book.

"I lost it," he said.

"How is that possible?" I asked him. "Well, never mind. Tomorrow morning I'll visit the Pantherville library. They'll have a range of local phone books."

"I'd say they will," Boo said. "But I'll need the truck in the morning. I've got to load the dogs."

"Where are you taking them?"

"Not taking them anywhere. We're going to practice loading."

It was not my place to question that. It was frustrating, though, to think I'd be stuck on the knob all day when there was work to be done. I had noticed a bicycle on the carport behind a rack of shelves, and I asked Boo if I could use it.

"It's pink," he said.

"I don't care. I need transportation."

We went out to the carport and moved the rack of shelves and part of a bed frame and extracted the bike. It was a girl's one-speed bike with a pale pink frame and white tires and a basket on the front with plastic flowers on it.

"Maybe I do care," I said.

Boo dug around in a closet and found a can of flat black stove paint. I wiped the bike down with some dry paper towels to get the dust off and Boo hit it with a quick coat of black. "You want the basket gone?"

"I can use the basket," I said.

He nodded and silently nicked off the plastic daisy heads using his pocketknife.

The following morning I biked the two miles into town to visit the Pantherville branch of the county public library. It was located in what had formerly been a four-bay parking garage at the end of the building that also housed the volunteer fire department. Inside there were a few rows of shelves, a computer workstation, and behind the front desk, a red-haired librarian in her sixties. I approached and introduced myself, and I asked if the library had any special holdings on Andrew Johnson.

"Why, no," she said.

"I thought you might, because of the local connection."

"There is no local connection that I know of," she said.

"Andrew Johnson was from Greeneville," I said.

"That's correct."

"I wonder if you have a range of local phone books to which I might refer?" I said.

"I only have the library copies," she said.

"May I refer to them?"

"All of them?"

"I need to find all of the Jarvises," I said.

"You don't understand," she said quietly. "The telephone directories are not part of our holdings. They're for the use of library staff."

My gaze found the stack of three phone books on the countertop behind her, alongside the phone. Her gaze found my gaze, and she took a step sideways to block it.

The thing to understand when dealing with librarians is that there is not one among them who hasn't had her trust abused over the years. Art books with the illustrations razored out; pages of text with coffee, cocoa, or other, more mysterious fluids spilled over them; volumes dropped in the bath or simply never returned. No book was ever brought back in better condition than when it left the library. And yet it is the librarian's job to trust and trust again. They deserve some understanding and sympathy, and I've found that a little submissiveness goes a long way with them. I offered to leave my wallet at the desk while I made my photocopies.

"I don't think so," she said quietly.

I stepped across the room to have a quick look through Dewey sections 300 and 900, confirming that there was nothing in the collection of use to me. It looked like I'd need the truck after all: this trip had been totally unproductive. And yet, here is the funny way things happen. I looked into a back corner of the room, behind some shelves, where a small used-book sale had been set up, and there I found several back issues of *Civil War Days* laid out for a nickel apiece. I picked one up and flipped to the masthead. There was my name, third down from the top: proof that I had existed.

I laid the magazine back on the stack. Perhaps some young person would buy them, a boy or girl whose interest in the American past would be kindled.

I turned to go and was startled to find the librarian standing directly behind me. "If you see something you want, you'd better buy it now before Jeffa throws it out," she said.

I gathered the whole stack up and carried it to the front. While passing the computer workstation I saw there was a person at the keyboard. I hadn't noticed her before, hunkered behind the screen. To my surprise, I recognized her: it was Danielle McBain, the New Yorker I had met in Greeneville three days earlier. Even more strangely, she winked at me.

I set the magazines down on the librarian's desk.

"Now how many have you chosen?" she said, sitting.

"Twenty-one," I said.

The librarian started counting in a loud whisper.

From behind the computer came snickering.

The librarian stopped counting and gave a long *"Shh-hhhhhhhhhhhh."*

"Am I being shushed?" McBain said from behind the computer.

The librarian paused, then resumed her counting. I

produced a dollar and five cents in warm change from my pocket. I arranged the coins edgewise between my thumb and first finger, hoping they'd cool to room temperature before it was time to hand them over.

"Damn, this connection is slow!" McBain said.

"There will be no more speaking in the library," the librarian said.

McBain stood. "There's no one else here," she said. "You're counting, he's standing, I'm waiting on my e-mail to send—we're it! There's no one here to disturb."

"Mrs. Fletcher is here and she's trying to read," the librarian said. She nodded towards an ancient small lady standing with a walker beside a bookcase that was nearly twice her height. She was the second person I hadn't noticed in this library. Even now, when her name was spoken, she didn't look up or take a step. She was smiling into a book, her forearms at rest on the rails of her walker. Her head bobbled slightly.

McBain grabbed her purse and walked past me towards the exit. But then she circled past some chairs and stepped up directly behind Mrs. Fletcher. McBain clapped her hands. Mrs. Fletcher didn't move.

"This woman is deaf!" McBain said.

The librarian stood. "You must leave now!" she said.

McBain leveled a finger at me. "You! You saw—she didn't flinch, did she?"

I didn't answer. I had dropped my change and was retrieving it from the carpet.

"I'm lifting the phone to call the sheriff," the librarian said.

"Talking is not a crime," McBain said. She left the library, swinging her arms.

Still holding the receiver, the librarian turned her attention to me.

"Twenty-one, I believe," I said. "One dollar five cents. Thank you very much."

She scowled at me, and I took my magazines and left.

I found McBain waiting outside. "Why are you in Pantherville? Are you following me?" she said.

"No. I live here."

"Oh. Well you've got a hell of a lot of nothing going on here," she said. "I've been whinnied at, and now I've been shushed, and that's about all the excitement I've seen."

"Have you not found your four-handed babies?" I said.

"No. The four-handed babies are not materializing. I found a girl with seven fingers whose mother is very eager to get her on television, but I had to tell the lady, seven fingers just isn't that unusual."

"Seven fingers total?"

"Twelve total. Seven and five."

Now that we were outside the library, I noticed, McBain's voice had gone much quieter. I had to stand close to hear her.

"I've spent too much time and money here to leave with nothing," she said.

"There was a fractious anti-income-tax demonstration in Nashville this week," I said.

"Hm. Did anybody get killed? I'm half joking."

"Then the legislature scheduled a referendum on amending the state constitution to allow a lottery."

She nodded. "That's not really very interesting," she said.

"On the contrary. These are important decisions about how the people of a state will invest and provide—"

"There has to be a story," she said, cutting me off. "You're talking about political science, which is a subject people study in college, and that's not why people switch on the television. When they switch on the television, they want news in the form of a little tale."

"A little tale?"

"Right. Strong characters, the clash of interests—and there has to be some twist in it. A zinger. Some little sick thing you never thought of before."

"I thought journalists reported news," I said.

"We package it," she said.

I considered briefly, then spoke. "The referendum wouldn't have passed the House except that our local representative was tricked into voting in favor of it."

"What do you mean, 'tricked'?"

"A lobbyist confused him at the last minute," I said. "I know this representative. He's a clerk at the local post office. He got faked out, so to speak."

"What's his name?"

"Ron Runnels. As I say, we're acquainted."

Her eyes narrowed slightly. The gratification I felt was accompanied by shame. So I had done the impossible: I had impressed a New Yorker.

"He told you this?" McBain asked.

"I can't tell you any more without breaking a confidence," I said.

"Judging by the look on your face, you've already broken the confidence," she said. "Now just tell me whose confidence you broke."

"No, I'm sorry. I shouldn't have said anything."

"Why did you, then?"

I was quiet.

She backed up a step, then came in closer. "Look here," she said. "I want to let you know something, or maybe remind you of something you already know. Do you know who Robert Redford is?"

"Yes."

"And have you seen a certain movie by the title of *All the President's Men?*"

"Yes."

"Okay. Let's think for a minute in terms of the service hard journalism provides us in a republic, which by the way is our form of government in this country. Remind me of your name."

"John Tolley," I said. "That film was based on a book."

"I'm aware it was! I simply remind you of the name of Robert Redford because most people associate him with the story more readily than they do those other two journalists, whose names are often forgotten! That's how it is for us—we work behind the scenery, not for fame but to get at the truth. Now, the truth is something bigger than you, John Tolley, and it is bigger than the privacy or confidence of one person. And if you know someone who can expose dubious or corrupt activities by officials of the Tennessee government, it is your responsibility as a Tennessean to name that person now."

"I'm not a Tennessean," I said. "And on the contrary, there is nothing wrong with keeping an informant's name confidential. What about Deep Throat?"

I had won the point, though I was not at all sure that she knew it. She was right about the other thing, though: I had already broken the confidence.

She was picking through her purse, which was made of a hard, smooth, highly polished black leather and which was surprisingly small and slender, I thought, for the purse of a woman who was traveling. She produced a tiny cell phone and studied the display.

"Do you have to go?" I said.

"Eventually, yes. Let me tell you one thing, Tolley. In nothing I do am I concerned with the advocacy of one side over another. I have a different loyalty, one which some people find odd because it is unusual. My allegiance is to a funny thing known as reality. Do you know what reality is?"

"The question can be answered in more than one way," I said.

She blinked at me. "I have to have a cigarette now," she said. She pulled a square tin from her purse. It held a single layer of about twenty cigarettes side by side. She set one between her thin lips, which were outlined in brown pencil. Suddenly she looked up, as though only then noticing that we stood in the sun, and she made an anguished face and took three steps sideways into the shade of a low sugar maple. She lit up and took a long drag, then exhaled, looking interested by her thoughts.

She took another drag, then threw her cigarette to the ground and stepped on it. She then knelt in one smooth motion, her thin legs clamped closely together in her tailored skirt, and picked up the butt from the mulch. She rose and dropped the butt into a wastebasket. "What are you looking at?" she asked me.

I felt my chin move, but I didn't speak. I looked at her spotless black shoes, with their toes shaped like playing cards.

A white Wagoneer pulled into the parking area and Dweena Price got out. I raised an arm and she waved back at me, sort of. McBain and I watched her unlock the front of a blue mailbox and drag the mail into a plastic tub. She slid the tub into the back of the Wagoneer and left.

"Have I met her?" McBain said.

"How would I know?"

"Has she modeled?"

"Again, I have no way of knowing, though I would be very surprised to learn that she had."

"She's striking," McBain said.

"You think she's attractive?"

"Sure, why not? Possibly I have seen her in magazines."

"I don't think so," I said. "This isn't Manhattan, with celebrities crawling in every direction. And even if she were a model, she wouldn't be in the sorts of magazines you read."

"Don't be so sure," McBain said. "I read widely."

"You haven't read Woodward and Bernstein," I said.

But she wasn't listening. She got into a silver Taurus and backed it up, then powered down the passenger-side window to speak to me. I missed the first part of what she was saying—something about a "bucket of fresh spring greens."

"I beg your pardon?" I said.

"I said there's no edible food here and I may starve," she said. "Anyway here's this. Knock yourself out, kid." She pulled some folded papers from her purse and tossed them at me, then whipped the car in a backwards arc across the parking lot and was gone.

I picked up the papers from where they had landed on the pavement and unfolded them. They were pages from three separate telephone directories, each torn neatly from the J section.

14

I RODE THE BICYCLE BACK to Boo's place. Pedaling up Jasper Price Road, I saw white smoke rising from behind the barn. I rode around back. There was Boo, tending a fire on the ground, with Brownie lying in the grass at a safe distance, basking. "Hello Mr. Tolley," Boo said.

"What are you burning?" I said.

"Trash."

Yellow papers were scattered across the ground. He fed them into the fire one by one.

"May I borrow your phone?" I said.

"You may."

There were ninety-eight Jarvises in the three separate listings. I called and spoke with Mr. Asger Jarvis of Kingsport, who told me he had no relation that he knew of to any former president, nor was he kin to anyone named Edna. I thanked him, hung up, and drew a careful line through his name.

I was about to dial again when the phone rang under my hand. It was Boo.

"John, will you bring a hose across the road?" he said. I heard Brownie barking.

"Where are you calling from?" I said.

"The cell phone. Hurry up please," he said.

I found the hose and ran with it across the road. The fire had gotten high, and ash and bits of flaming paper were rising in an updraft towards the silvered planks of the barn. "Just hose down that wall if you would," Boo said to me. He was beating out a small grass fire with a piece of tin.

I did as he instructed. Near my foot was one of the yellow papers, still intact, and though I had deliberately not looked at them before, I picked this one up and read it. I saved it, and I insert it here:

DID YOU KNOW???

. . . State lotteries is a Tax on hope?

. . . the Tennessee Constitution has forbid them since 1796?

. . . you stand a better chance of being drafted by the NBA than of winning Megamillions?

. . . a slick glad-handing lobbyist strokes your elected representatives?

. . . gambling is a Bible Sin, no matter how you slice it?

. . . the wages of sin is

Painful
DEATH?

Their Foot Shall Slide. Meanwhile, vote No for the Tennessee lottery.

"Paid for by Upright Tennesseans Thinking Of The Children"

The page had been folded once and was stamped, on the outside, "Non Profit Org., U.S. Postage Paid."

"Boo, this is mail!" I said.

"No it's not," he said.

"It appears to be!"

He set down his piece of tin and came over to where I was standing with the hose. He took off his cap, rubbed his head, and put his cap back on. "You weren't strictly supposed to see this, John," he said. "Will you do me a favor and put it out of your mind?"

"That's not easy to do," I said.

"But you can do it if you try," Boo said.

"Instead of spraying the barn, why don't we just spray the fire out?" I said.

"I'm enjoying the fire," Boo said.

I sprayed it out.

"Well, that's done," he said. He took the hose from me and gave Brownie a drink from it. Then we walked back across the road to turn the water off.

"I see you got some magazines," Boo said.

I had parked the bike by the carport with the magazines in the basket. I told Boo this was the magazine I had worked for in Ohio. He picked up a copy and opened it to a full-page color ad for the "Horses of the Civil War" plate set.

"Nice," he said. He sat down at the patio table and flipped through the pages, back to front.

I went inside and called thirty Jarvises. It was slow work and not pleasant. I was annoying people in their homes. I pressed on for the better part of the afternoon, though, until I was quaking with hunger. I asked Boo what he had to eat.

"Need to go to the store," he said. He was still reading magazines but had moved to the living room.

"Let's go up to the knob and get some food," I said.

"Need to feed and tend these dogs first," he said.

I followed him out back and sprayed out the runs while he measured the food. Each dog did not get a cupful. One dog got two-thirds of a cup, and the next got three-fourths. All took supplements, too, but not the same supplements. Some were liquid, and some were powder. One took pieces of what looked like chopped pepperoni in his food. Boo fed the dogs three times a day.

The dogs had adopted Boo's bearing, or perhaps he had bred them selectively for it. The bearing was alert and mostly unflappable. There was a little note of defeat in it somewhere. When Boo stepped up to the gate of a run, the dog that was in it stood. Boo let himself in and set the stainless steel bowl with the food in it onto the concrete, and the dog would then step up to him and wait to have its ears and shoulders rubbed vigorously for half a minute or so while Boo praised it. Then Boo backed out of the run, and the dog would go to its bowl. When the last dog had its food, Boo stood back and watched them all eat. He was absorbed in this spectacle, even though he had watched it every day, three times a day, since shortly after his release from the state penitentiary in Brushy Mountain, Tennessee. While the dogs were eating he didn't smile, hum, sniff, or speak. He simply watched the dogs.

Then we hiked up the hill and I prepared a double batch of Tuna Helper, which we gobbled down while reading magazines. In addition to the copy of *Civil War Days* he was working through, he had brought a magazine called *Nose Dog* for me to look at. It had coon-hunting pictures and stories, and studying it gave me a better sense of what this activity was all about. I asked Boo about the title of the magazine and he explained that there are nose dogs and eye dogs. His dogs were nose dogs, he said.

"I suppose there are ear dogs as well," I said.

"Ear dogs?" He laughed for some time.

I was at the sink washing up dishes when there was a loud knock at the door. Boo went to get it, and a moment later Danielle McBain strode into the kitchen. She stopped in the middle of the floor and raised her face, not looking but apparently smelling in one direction then another. Her thin arms hung like straightened coat hangers. "So this is where John Tolley lives," she said.

Boo resumed his seat and went back to his magazine.

"How did you find me?" I said.

"I'm sneaky this way."

"It doesn't take much skill to tail a man who's riding a bicycle," I said.

"You're wrong there," she said. "I had a line of pick-ups backed up behind me."

Boo nodded without looking up. "If you didn't see her from a bike, she's good," he said.

"So, Tolley, have you been phoning your Jarvises?"

"Yes I have," I said.

"You're welcome for that bit of assistance."

"I don't thank you, because I don't approve of tearing out pages."

"I didn't think you did. That's why I did it for you. Why do you have to talk to all of the Jarvises in all of the phone books anyway?"

"I'm looking for a particular Jarvis who is related to Andrew Johnson," I said.

"I see. Come take a ride with me now, okay?"

"Where?"

"I don't know. Around," she said.

"Don't worry about me, John," Boo said. "I'm fine here with my magazine."

I went with her. Why, I couldn't have said. We got into a green Taurus. "What happened to your silver Taurus?" I asked.

"I switched rentals," she said. "It'd been seen. I had lunch with your friend Ronnie Runnels today."

"You did? How did you meet him?"

"Small town—we ran into each other. Anyway, what's with him? Was he knocked on the head?"

"I don't know," I said. "I think he's just not very bright."

"Worse than not bright. He's an absolute sock monkey. Did you know he never ran for office? He was installed there by county honchos."

"That's public knowledge," I said. "When a legislator resigns or dies, the Board of Supervisors appoints his replacement."

"Right. Well there's one of those guys, the one who

got Runnels appointed, who now tells him what to do in Nashville. The puppet master."

"One of the supervisors?"

"Correct. He schedules Ronnie's trips, tells him how to vote, everything. Well, other people tell him how to vote, too, but this Dwayne is the main one."

"Dwayne?"

"Dwayne. He's on the Board of Supervisors. A gigantic county honcho. And here's tonight's lead—they're holding a major powwow this evening. All these good ol' Billy Bobs are gathering up for some very crucial assembly that Runnels assures me is top, top secret. Everyone of importance will be there."

"If it's so secret, why did he tell you about it?" I said.

She grinned. "Because he literally does not know what he's doing, do you see? He's a child."

"Does he know you're a TV news producer?"

"Sure!"

"But does he understand the implications? Does he know what a producer does?"

"Not a clue of it! Look, if you're asking me am I taking advantage of his wanting intelligence, the answer is yes. Do you expect me to hire him an attorney? Because I'm not going to do that. This is journalism, not the Idiot's Defense Fund. So we're following him tonight."

"Following him where?"

"I don't know! If I knew, we wouldn't follow. We would meet him there!"

I was quiet for a time. She drove us into Pantherville, and we stopped in the parking lot of the Pantherville

Store. She pointed to a small frame house set far back from the road, with a birdbath in the yard. "The Runnels home," she said.

"Why am I here?" I said.

"I need you. While I'm driving, sometimes you'll sit up, but then sometimes you'll hunch down. I've also got some hats for you to wear."

"If that's all I'm needed for, count me out," I said.

She shrugged. "Okay, you're out."

"Take me home," I said.

"I can't leave. He may appear at any moment."

We sat for an hour, and then an orange Chevrolet pickup turned off the road and went up the driveway to Runnels's house. It honked. I of course knew the truck, but said nothing. Runnels emerged from the house on his crutches. He laid them in the truck bed and got in front.

We followed the truck out of Pantherville and onto one of the winding two-lane state highways where I so easily got turned around. I had been on this one before, though, on the drive to Greeneville. A maroon pickup pulled between us and the orange pickup, and McBain swore roughly. She flicked the wheel, switching us into the left lane to pass, but a small car came over a crest and she had to swerve right to miss it. I had eaten my fill of tuna with noodles, and I suddenly felt sick. When the little car had gone by, McBain veered left again and stomped the accelerator, and we got past the maroon pickup. She told me to duck. I balked, and she shoved me down.

"If I can't see the horizon I will vomit," I said.

"Take steady breaths," she said.

I found the lever under the seat and moved the seat as far back as it would go. "Am I visible?" I said.

"Keep the top of that head down," she said.

I twisted around so that my back was against the door, and my left knee was on the car seat. It's a little hard to describe the position. Ms. McBain's thin trunk, in an off-white silk blouse, was directly in front of my face. The fabric caught the late, low sun like reflector tape. She steered with both hands on the wheel. With nothing else to look at, I imagined how the ribs must jut from her narrow barrel of a chest. She was a lean, sugar-burning type. She had so little flesh on her bones, I supposed it must hurt her to sit on a wooden chair.

"Where in the hell are we going?" she demanded to know.

"You're astin me?"

She ignored my response, which was a quote from my old boss Terence Choate, who when he did not know the answer to a question, or was too bored to properly answer the question, would reply, "You're astin me?" Sometimes on a quiet afternoon he would say the phrase unprompted, even though no one had asted him anything.

McBain was not wearing stockings. The skin along the fronts of her shins was shiny. She worked her small white ankles energetically, braking hard then gassing hard again to make up for overbraking. I felt ill and sorry, yet interested. I scooted my way back up into the seat.

"What are you doing?" McBain said. She laid her hand on my shoulder, trying to shove me back down.

"I have to get a look out the window or be sick," I said.

"We're in the crunch now and you've got to stay calm," she said.

"I'm calmly going to throw up."

"Climb in back," she said. "Hurry."

I pulled my foot up into the seat and launched myself towards the back. My wing tip caught the parking brake, though. The wheels locked and the car lurched then went into a skid. My body was flung on top of Danielle McBain's.

We came to a stop in the middle of the road. My torso was wedged between Ms. McBain's back and her backrest. She jabbed my thigh a few times, and I climbed off of her and on into the back seat.

Out the rear window, I saw the maroon pickup that we had passed earlier come to an easy stop behind us. It was a clean Dodge of 1970s vintage. In the cab were an elderly couple, the man in a hat with a herringbone pattern. He and his wife watched from a safe distance as McBain got the rented Taurus pointed in the right direction.

She gunned the engine to catch up with the orange Chevy, and then we rounded a sharp turn and were right on top of it. The truck had slowed down to pull into a gravel driveway that was lined with honeysuckle and wild rose bushes. We went on by, McBain craning her neck to watch where the pickup had gone, and I noticed she had blood on her lip. "You're bleeding," I said.

"So what," she said. I offered my handkerchief, and she took a look at it—it was clean—and shook her head. "We need to ditch this car."

We crossed a short bridge, then she pulled onto a pair of dirt ruts that led us down to the creek below. We stopped. I asked her what her plan was.

"We're going back to see what they're up to," she said.

"It'll be dark soon."

"We want it to be dark," she said. "Hand me my bag."

I passed a leather shoulder bag up to her. She pulled out a tissue and dabbed at her mouth. I asked her was it quite usual for television news producers to be following people on highways and creeping up their driveways during the night and so forth. Was this the sort of thing she often did? She said yes, it was perfectly ordinary behavior for her and for all top-tier television journalists. "It's a highly competitive business in which we push all of the limits, all of the time."

"Who's your competition tonight?" I said. "We're on the side of a creek in Tennessee."

"Let's philosophize later," she said. "Hop out while I change."

I got out and stood on some sandy ground with my back to the car, looking into the clear, quick-moving water. There were big rocks in the stream—giant, angular chunks of gray limestone. How had they gotten there? I asked myself. They'd been dragged there by farmers, perhaps, clearing the bottom land for cultivation.

McBain appeared dressed in tight black nylon shorts, a sweatshirt, and running shoes. She saw me looking and said, "That was a three-hundred-dollar skirt, Skateboard."

"Did you call me 'Skateboard'?" I said.

"Yes. I'm not wild about the name 'John.'"

"I've never been on a skateboard in my life," I said.

We stood around a bit while the sky got dark, then walked. McBain had brought a small flashlight. We crossed the bridge, walked a short ways up the highway, then turned up the driveway where the orange Chevy had gone. We hadn't gotten far when gravel crunched behind us. McBain shoved me one way into the bushes, and she went the other way. I lay flat until the pickup had gone by. Then I raised my head and saw McBain jogging away after the pickup.

I got up and followed her, my eyes on her white shoes and calves. There was a bit of a moon out. I heard a horse nickering.

We stopped in a clump of trees. Up ahead there was a long barn or shed made of corrugated metal. Five pickups and a couple of cars were lined up outside it, and a light showed along the eaves.

"Why would they meet in a barn?" McBain said.

"Let's catch our breath and think awhile," I said.

She ran out of the trees towards the barn. I watched her go. She paused behind a truck, crouching. She didn't look back at me once. I got up and ran to join her.

"There's a dog chained by the front of the barn," I said.

"I don't see it." She switched on a flashlight.

"Be careful!" I said.

She switched it off. "Okay, I see the dog," she said. "We'll go around this way." She jogged far wide of the building, off to the right, and I followed.

We circled behind the barn then came up close, past a

baler and a hay rake and a tedder in a row. There was a pair of big sliding doors, and a chain with a padlock had been run through two holes cut into the metal. McBain and I moved up close and peered through the narrow gap between the doors.

We saw a dozen people standing inside, men and some boys, most of them with their backs to us. The floor was dirt, and fluorescent light fixtures hung from the roof trusses. I spotted Dwayne Loupe, who was tallest. A man gave a yell, and some others laughed.

"I don't know what this is," McBain said in my ear. "This is not what I was expecting."

"Maybe they're grilling food," I said.

There was a sort of pen around which they had gathered. Runnels was inside the pen. Then he limped out of it through a gate, carrying something under his arm. The other men stepped aside to let him pass, and he came away from them towards the back of the barn, directly towards us, hobbling without his crutches. The thing he was carrying was about the size of a football, and he held it away from him now to see it better under the lights. Whatever it was, it was limp, and a strong, thin stream of blood was draining from it.

After studying the thing briefly he reached his arm across it, made a fist, and then flipped his fist, as though uncapping a bottle. He tossed the thing towards us, underhand. It skidded a few feet on the dusty, smooth floor and was still for a moment; then it popped up off of the floor by itself and tumbled away in a long, tousled commotion of feathers, wings, and scaly-toed feet.

"It's a chicken!" McBain said. We both backed away from the gap.

The expression on her face—which I could see, though not well, in a vertical bar of light—was an expression of bitter savor. "They're practicing Santeria!" she said.

"I don't think that's it," I said.

"I think it is! This whole world of Tennessee is creeping me out very deeply," she whispered. "I don't know if I can put this on television or not. Well, what am I saying? Of course I can." She put her eye back to the gap. "The chicken is still now," she said. "What's that thing on its foot?"

I looked. "It looks like a small knife," I said. It appeared to be fastened to the bird's leg.

"It *is* a knife! This isn't voodoo, it's a *chicken fight!*"

"Let's go," I said.

She raised her hand to silence me. "That big guy holding the coffee cup, that's Dwayne," she said. "I saw him today, too. He runs the post office as well as being a sultan of the county. And the blond guy is Runnels's roommate."

"His roommate?"

"Yep. Just like college days."

I looked again. It was the blond man I had seen with Dwayne Loupe and Boo, dumping the yellow flyers. I didn't know what to make of this. Someone handed the blond man a chicken, and he lifted it up in front of his own face and stared hard at its head. Then he turned it around and blew into its hind feathers.

A white flash went off. Some of the men looked up at the fluorescent bulbs overhead.

McBain backed away from the doors. She was holding a disposable camera.

"What are you doing?" I said.

She waved the camera. "I took a picture!"

"Be quiet!"

"I won't be quiet!" she said. "I'm on this now. I'm on top of the darn case, little man." She tucked the camera into a pocket of her sweatshirt and strode away from me towards the corner of the barn.

"Not that way," I said. *"The dog."*

She didn't answer but spun around and held something up from her other pocket that jingled—a key ring, I thought.

I stepped after her. "Come on, let's go the long way," I said.

A voice said, *"Youns are going nowhere."*

McBain stopped short. The person who had spoken stepped out from behind the baler and clamped a hand over her wrist. She tried to pull away, but he held tight. From his free hand, a blade glinted.

15

"LET GO OF THAT LADY," I said.

"Do what?"

He was a young man of about my height, though brawnier. "I said let go of her!"

"You're hurting my wrist!" McBain said. "If you damage my wrist I will sue!"

He dropped her wrist and took a step back. "I thought you was a boy!" he said.

Now I learned what it was that McBain had showed me from her pocket. It was a small spray canister on her key ring. She had brought it out for the dog, but now she used it on her human assailant, spraying him long and thoroughly over the face. She moved her arm side to side like Johnny Bench in the old spray-paint commercial: "No runs, no drips, no errors." The boy brought a hand to his eyes. McBain snapped his picture, then ran.

I stepped up next, kicking him with accuracy in the forearm. The heavy-soled wing tip found his ulna and struck it with force. The knife went to the ground, and I took it.

The boy groaned. He clutched his arm now and rocked himself, his weeping eyes squeezed shut. "What have you people done to me?" he said.

"You'll survive."

"I'm in pain! Where's my knife at?" He sunk to the ground and patted with his hands.

"I've got the knife now," I said.

"Give it back!"

"I don't think I will."

"My papaw give me that knife and told me stories about it!"

It was an old Barlow. "Now I have a story about the knife," I said. I closed it and slid it into my pocket.

He whimpered, then drew in a long breath. "Hey, Tate!" he yelled. "We're being spied on!"

Around front, the dog began barking. I ran.

The grass was to my knees. I had chosen a different direction than McBain, improving the odds that at least one of us would escape. I ran rather wildly, as fast as I could, and I had looked back over my shoulder when something brought me down and began beating me silly. It was another electric fence. This time, it wasn't stiff wire but a narrow, flexible tape that got looped around my leg.

What followed were the longest thirty seconds of my life. The shock was not steady but periodic, like water dripping. Each jolt was like being whipped across the body with two-by-fours. Finally I managed to slither free, and I lay quivering like a wet newborn pup, helpless and blind. Not only had I been seriously and repeatedly shocked, but I had thrashed my own limbs and head against the hard ground.

After a short time I got up and went on. I looped around the barn, and there I heard a truck start and saw its headlights swing around. I was guessing that McBain had run off the way we came in, along the driveway. If so, the men in the truck would soon find her—or else the dog would. If I kept on running the way I was headed, I thought I could probably wade the creek and get to the road undiscovered. Instead, though, I doubled back towards the driveway to get McBain.

I moved quickly, keeping my head down. In this posture I ran up against a board fence. It hurt, but I preferred it to the electric kind. I climbed the fence and dropped off the other side into thick, sticky mud. The truck was coming with its high beams on. The dog was barking viciously, but I took heart, reasoning that if it could bark it did not have McBain's thin calf in its jaws.

The truck came slowly. A boy leaned out of the open passenger-side door, swinging a powerful flashlight beam side to side. He lit up, from behind, a small shed, which I ran for. I crept up to it just as the pickup came alongside, and I slipped into the darkness.

Inside the shed, I heard huffing and some heavy steps, and then I felt a hot blast of breath in my face. It was followed by the loud, moist snort of a horse.

Outside, the truck stopped. The horse put her head out into the light and rolled her eye. She whinnied, raising her whiskery lip. "Hush old girl," the boy called. The cracks between the boards in the shed wall let in bars of light, by which I made out a black baby mule at the mare's side. At least now I knew where I was. The mule baby bobbed its slabby head. The truck moved along.

The mare backed up towards me suddenly, and both back legs came flying. One hoof hit the shed wall near my head with a splintering force. Without thinking, I dove to the ground. Hooves landed on every side, and another kick hit the shed wall. Then the mare bolted, and the baby mule tore off lightly behind her. They circled the lot at a gallop, the mare whipping a back leg out sideways from time to time, the mule with his big head finely aloft. The boy followed them with his light. While he watched them, I crawled through the mud and rolled under the bottom fence board into the grass along the driveway.

Now I got up and followed the truck. Of course, should the driver have looked back, he would have seen me in the taillights easily; so I ran up right behind the truck and crept along closely with my hand on the rear bumper and my head just below the top edge of the tailgate. Now I was out of their sight. Further, I had a good view from here of the field that the boy was searching. As he used his flashlight to look for McBain, so did I.

We didn't find her, though. At the foot of the driveway the driver punched the gas and left me behind. He swung back onto the main road, and I quickly dashed across and jumped into a ditch, where I lay down flat. The truck reversed, stopped short of running me over, and then threw gravel onto me as it headed back up the drive to search the opposite field.

I sat up. A thought occurred to me: McBain might well be hiding nearby, waiting for me to show up. I dared not raise my voice, so instead, I gave a long, warbling whistle that sounded very much like the call of a screech owl. I did this several times, until it occurred to me that perhaps my owl call sounded *too* real.

"Danielle," I hissed loudly. "Danielle."

A set of headlights appeared up the road, from across the bridge. They approached, swept over me briefly, and were gone. I watched the taillights recede.

Then the brake lights came on. The driver had seen me. The reverse lights lit up and the car backed up fast, engine whining. It stopped alongside me, and the passenger window powered down.

"Tolley, get in," McBain said.

I did, and she stood on the gas.

"Why were you in the ditch?" she said.

"I was trying to find you, of course."

"In a ditch?"

"I didn't know where you were. I didn't expect you to leave without me."

"I didn't leave without you," she said. "You're here."

"Only because you happened to pass me as you were leaving."

"I waited forever!"

"I'm sorry I held you up," I said.

"It's the past now."

"My clothing is soaked with ditch water. I expect I'll be coming down with malaria."

"We'll find you some quinine for that," she said.

"This here has been one extremely fruitful little junket, John Tolley."

"Slow down," I said.

"I need a tiny camera," she said. "Like a purse camera, or even smaller."

"What are you going to do with a purse camera?"

"Film them," she said. "We'll go back like tonight."

"No. Tonight's never being repeated," I said.

"Tonight *will* be repeated, on tape."

"No it won't. Anyway, why a purse camera? Are you going to hold your purse up to the crack between the doors?"

She stared at me briefly as though I were an alien creature. "We'll put a camera in my hair, then," she said. "Or we'll bring the whole damned van, with the lights and the tubbies and the cables and the whole damned satellite thing! This story's about to crack open for me, Tolley, you sad sack! You're going to see it happen! It's splitting open, it's dividing and ripening, and I'm going to eat it up and thrive on it, my friend. I glory!" She threw her arm out and hit me in the shoulder, and an inarticulate noise came out of her mouth.

I couldn't respond to this sort of display. I let it go by.

"Who can I call this minute?" she said. She reached for her purse in the floor and pulled out a cell phone, which she shook, flipping down the mouthpiece. She looked at it, then handed it to me. I held it and we rode in silence. I could all but observe the excited thoughts churning in a steamy cloud above her head. The cell phone was tiny—no broader than a business card. I closed it and slid it back into her purse.

She drove to the house on the knob and followed me in. I went to the kitchen to wash up. The backs of my hands were caked with dried mud, which tugged on the hairs as I scrubbed. My shirt was unsalvageable.

McBain stood in the kitchen doorway, watching me. "How did you get so dirty?" she said.

I chose not to answer.

"Is there something to drink?"

I told her she was welcome to whatever she found.

At the refrigerator, she removed the cap from a jug of water and sniffed at it, then put it back. She poured herself a large glass of apple juice. "Tonight exhilarated the hell out of me," she said. "I love my work."

"I don't."

She took several small gulps of her juice then set the glass in the sink. "But it's important work. Staging fights between chickens is illegal," she said. "And it's brutal as well. Did you see Runnels twist that bird's neck? He threw the thing down like a gym towel! This man is a lawmaker, sworn to uphold constitutions and so forth— and he's partaking of criminal enterprise along with common thugs!"

"Those men aren't thugs," I said. "They're farmers and mailmen."

"Farmers, mailmen, thugs, appointees—they're all going down, every one of them, before I'm finished. I'm throwing a barbecue cookout, John. *Family style.*"

"You're making too much out of this," I said.

She considered, smiling at her private thoughts.

"What's the story?" I asked.

"Now that's a pertinent question," she said. "Let us think. We have Runnels, a warm body in the Tennessee legislature. We have Dwayne, who captains a post office, and who also captains Runnels. We have a very biblically conservative neck of the woods, and we have a chicken fight. Chickens: they are placed in a large pen, with wire around it, a net of wire—*chicken wire!*—and the birds are put inside to kill each other. Why do they do that? The chickens, I mean?"

"Because they're bloodthirsty?"

She tilted her head. "But not for just any blood. For the blood of another male chicken. A rooster, also known as a cock."

"That's right," I said.

"Hormonal aggression. An urge to kill, to maim. They have knives strapped onto their legs. The trainers must train them to use the knives."

"I don't think they train them," I said. "The knives are just an improvement on the naturally occurring spurs."

"Spurs. I don't know what you're saying," she said.

I explained to her what a rooster spur is. I showed her on my ankle the spot where it grows. But the thought was too fantastic for McBain.

"I know better than that," she said. "I've seen chickens pretty up-close and I think I would know if they had crazy spears growing out of their legs."

"It's true," I said.

"How can I pitch this?"

"Pitch what?"

She'd been pacing, and now she stopped and faced me. She said, "I've been partly dishonest with you, Tolley. At present I'm not an employee of *Point Blank*. I was, but I no longer am."

"You lied?"

"It would have been true if I'd said it a week ago." She shrugged.

"What happened? You were fired?"

"No. My term was up. I was there on a kind of internship," she said.

"An internship? Is that true?"

"Okay, I was a temp," she said. "But look here. I was quite involved in many aspects of the operation of the place, due to the nature of my assignment. I worked *closely* with the producers and with *both* anchors. I was in meetings. I edited copy—nobody asked me to, but I did it on my own. I was fixing things constantly. That's what I did."

As I considered this new information, my understanding of everything connected to Danielle McBain began to change. I said, "Do you know that tonight I got an electric fence knotted around my leg?"

"You did?" She smiled, happy again. "What was that like?"

"I can't even begin to describe it," I said.

"I was thinking you seemed somehow different."

"Yes," I said. "It left an effect. Why are you here, and what do you want from me?"

"I'll take the first question first," she said. "I'm here, as I've told you, because of a tip. Someone called us."

"'Us'? Who are 'us'?"

"The show, *Point Blank*. People call all the time, from all over the country. 'My neighbors are killing dogs.' 'My barber is an organ thief.' 'I have nude pictures of Miss America.' And so on. You simply have no concept of the tips we get. It's quite frightening, believe me."

"There will always be crackpots," I said.

"These people aren't crackpots. They really do have nude pictures of Miss America."

"If you don't work for *Point Blank* anymore, why did they send you out on this tip?"

"No, John, look. They didn't send me. They never send anybody out on these tips."

"How did you get the tip, then?"

"I *took* the tip."

"You stole it?"

"No. I was a temp, John. I answered the telephone." She looked around the kitchen as though she had only now noticed it. "This place is primitive," she said. "Have you got any food?"

She opened a cupboard door. The shelves inside were full of books. "Oh my heavens," she said.

"You never saw a book before?"

"Sorry, what did you call it?" She took one down and opened it, bugging her eyes. *"B-b-book? What is book?"*

"These are the only shelves in the house," I said.

She set the book on the counter—it was a copy of the current *Chicago Manual of Style*—and opened more doors. There were books in every cupboard. "Where do you hide your food?" she said.

"You saw the refrigerator."

"*Icebox*," she said. "We like to say *icebox* in Tennessee. So, Tolley—do you read these books?"

"Of course I read them. What else am I going to use them for?"

"Have you read them all?"

"They're not décor," I said.

She raised her eyebrows in a way that was meant to convey admiration. Whether the admiration was genuine I could not have said. Perhaps Ms. McBain herself did not know. She pulled out another book and opened it, and a blue envelope fell out and hit the linoleum with a loud *clack*. The *clack* was unreproduceable: drop the same envelope a hundred times, and you would not hear that perfect sharp report again. McBain picked up the envelope and pulled out the contents.

"'Happy Birthday,'" she read. She flipped the card open. "'Dave Tolley.' Who's that, your cousin?"

"My father," I said. "He's deceased."

She nodded. "Odd that he signs his full name, instead of 'Dad' or something."

"That's how he signed it," I said.

"Was this card to you?"

"Yes, it was to me. It was my birthday."

"Did you call your father by his first name?"

"No. He signed everything that way."

She studied the signature again, and then she carefully placed the card back inside the envelope and back in the book, and she slid the book back into its place in the cupboard.

"That was kind of private," she said. "How old were you when he died?"

"I was twelve."

"And what did he do for a living?"

"He was a welder in Tampa."

"Good with his hands, then?"

"He didn't weld with his feet."

"Did he sign that card with his feet?"

"He wasn't good with a pen," I said.

"Who taught him to sign his name? Did you?"

"I did, as a matter of fact. Not for the purpose of signing that card, but to sign other things. Is that interesting to you?"

"Yes, it is interesting."

"Would you like to make a television show about it?"

"I don't know if it's *that* interesting," she said. "It tells me something about your story, though."

"My story is private. You're not here to learn my story, and neither am I."

"I'm not sure what you mean by that."

"I'm here to learn about Andrew Johnson," I said. "The *former president*. The seventeenth president, to be exact, and the first to be impeached. And you're here to dig up any sort of scandal so you can go back to New York and possibly get a job with a cable news show, though not in front of the camera."

"Ouch," she said. I hadn't hurt her, though. She wanted me to think I had.

"Let's try to keep this in its proper channel," I said.

She came a step closer. "Let's do that."

I put up a hand. "I'd like to be left alone now, please," I said.

"Fine, John. That's fine." She backed away. "Let me leave you with a thought, though. Chickens have rights, too."

"No they don't," I said.

"Of course they do! They have the right to live, and to——"

I cut her off. "A right is a thing that's articulated by those who possess it," I said. "For example, the Declaration of Independence and the UN's Universal Declaration of Human Rights were composed by human beings, and they describe human rights as humans understand them. There is no Chicken Declaration of Chicken Rights."

She glared at me. "Leaving that aside, though I don't concede——will you agree we're a nation of laws?"

"That's the idea," I said.

"All right then. When one in the public trust breaks the law, that makes him *what*? He's not one of us anymore. He must be crucified. Or——hey, look here!" Her eyes flashed. "Why do people watch chickens fight?"

"A terrible, vicious boredom is my guess."

"They place money on those fights," she said.

"Maybe they do."

"You know they do! Which is gambling, which is also what a lottery is." She threw both her hands in the air, as though that settled it.

"I don't know what you're talking about," I said.

"Let me spell it out for you, then. Conspiracy!"

I poured myself some water and drank it. I asked McBain, if she had no fancy network job, where was she getting the money for her rental car and travel expenses?

"A little thing called BankOne Visa," she said.

I asked her where she'd gone to college.

"Fayetteville. You were thinking Yale? I'm working my way up like you are."

Fayetteville—that did surprise me. "How does a native New Yorker wind up at the University of Arkansas?"

"I'm not a native New Yorker," she said.

"New Jersey?"

"I'm from Little Rock."

"You're from Arkansas?"

She nodded. "Borned and bred," she said.

This stunned me. I was speechless.

She was looking at the floor, and then she looked up at me and laughed. "My vowels are good, aren't they?"

"They're perfect."

"Thanks. First on our street to get television, and all that."

I didn't know what to think now. I was thrown. I'll admit to a shiver of envy.

"Look, John," she said. "I need your help. First, to keep quiet, and not tell anyone what we've seen. Second, to help me figure this out. Don't you kind of see we're on the same project, here? It's about the search for truth in a democratic society. The stakes are nothing less than the integrity of our constitutional system of government. You perceive the crucial importance here, right?"

"I don't think you really believe all of that," I said.

She shrugged. "Even if I don't, you still do."

16

I DIDN'T SLEEP WELL THAT NIGHT. There was scratching inside the wall above my bed, and my head was full of disorganized thoughts. I imagined I saw pivoting headlights, and my ears hummed with the stiff cadences of Andrew Johnson's presidential correspondence: *In compliance with the resolution of the House of Representatives of the twelfth ultimo and its request of the twenty-eighth instant for all correspondence, reports, and information in my possession in relation to the riot which occurred in the city of New Orleans on the 30th day of July last, I transmit herewith copies of telegraphic dispatches on the subject. . . .*

A bit of dust landed on my cheek, and I batted it away. I thought I smelled the curious spiciness of Mrs. Chouri's cooking.

I found myself thinking for the first time in years of a man named Gary Delp who once occupied the office next door to ours in Galena. We were in a small building alongside and slightly below the four-lane—*Civil War Days* had shared it with various tenants over the years, including a chiropractor, a series of accountants, and the local Green Party headquarters.

Gary Delp was one of the accountants. He couldn't have been much past fifty when I knew him, but his hair was solid white. He had a peculiarly boyish stride with a bounce in it, almost like skipping. We knew his walk well, because every day at eleven-thirty we would see him out our window, hiking up the frontage road and then across the four-lane to a Wendy's restaurant, where he ate a salad. Terence and I often ran into him there. At first, we invited him to ride back with us in Terence's car. "Oh no," Delp replied in his perky, dazed way. "I wouldn't trade my daily walk for a car ride if you gave me twenty dollars."

"Why would we give him twenty dollars to ride with us?" Terence said as he drove us back to the office.

"We wouldn't," I said.

"Delp is an oddball," Terence said. Later we started getting e-mail messages from Delp, long ones with lots of asterisks in them, describing what Delp considered to be noteworthy changes in the tax code, or sometimes keeping us up-to-date on the activities of the Galena Venturing Club, of which he was a member. The messages went out to dozens of recipients. They became a joke in our office, as did his daily hike across the four-lane. Terence mimicked his walk on trips to the coffeemaker. Then one day while going to Wendy's, Gary Delp slipped in some mud on the median and broke his ankle. He couldn't get up. He waved and shouted at cars, propped on one elbow, but the cars kept passing. After some time an Ohio State Highway Patrol officer stopped, and then an ambulance came. Terence and I missed the whole thing. We had gone for Chinese food that day, and we got the details later from a Green who had visited Delp in the hospital.

Delp recovered and even put the trademark bounce in his stride again, but his venturing days were over. He brought his lunch in a bag after that. Later he went out of business.

After an hour or two of thinking these thoughts and not sleeping, I got out of bed. A feeling of melancholy was on me. I wondered what ever became of Gary Delp, CPA. If you saw him in the hallway he would chatter on for minutes about taxes and indoor rock climbing, but mention some topic of interest to yourself and he had to run off to the copier, quick. It made him a difficult person to like. The last time I saw him he was loading his hatchback with cardboard file boxes, smiling through tears. "Gone bust!" he said. "But I'll bounce back!"

In spite of his eager beaverism, Gary Delp had struck me as ineffectual. I could think of nothing sadder. The world is a vast, teeming field of doers and strivers, where the ineffectual subside and are forgotten. They contribute a thing called humus to the soil.

I went to the kitchen and pulled down the volume that had the birthday card in it. My father, though not educated, was not an ineffectual man. He was skilled in a trade that is more complicated and delicate than most people know. He did well in it, though his inability to keep books or apply for a business license meant that he would always punch a clock in someone else's shop. He never complained—certainly not in my presence. Mother did. To her credit, though, as my father said, "She is not one to complain and do nothing."

The summer after my fifth-grade year she left for Texas, and soon after that she sought her first divorce. She'd found a man in Beaumont whose prospects impressed her. They got married, and then she brought him to Tampa to retrieve me.

There was no shouting, no smashing of things. My father and the new man stood in the yard together while Mother packed my clothes in plastic bags. From the window where I watched them, it appeared that the Texan was doing most of the talking. I suppose he had more to explain.

An accident on the job, the following December, is how my father died. The card had come a few weeks before that. We had worked on the signature during the summer when my mother was gone, and he had been practicing since.

I was glad to have this bit of his handiwork to carry with me. I saw his touch in it—the steady hand, the short, heavy, careful strokes. They were little marks that, when you studied them, became letters. He had sharpened his pencil with a knife, and the resulting flat tip gave its character to the line.

I thought of my own handwriting, which I like. I am a person who keeps his driver's license facedown in his wallet so he won't have to look at the picture, and yet whenever I see my handwriting I feel a sense of warm recognition and affection for myself. That is vanity. Then I thought of Shirley Walls's narrow cursive, upright and regular, a little old-ladyish. I had gotten to know it well in our journal-sharing days. The color of her eyes escaped me now, but I could see her marginalia as though it were there in front of me.

> *Excellent point, this.*
> *Specious reasoning.*
> *Specious.*

That had been a form of courtship, perhaps. Possibly I had been guilty of pretending not to understand. Twice a week for four years I had rapped on her screen door, causing her cockatiel to shriek and scatter its seed.

There are many people in the world, I thought. Six billion upright bipeds—quite an accumulation, and a head on every one with thoughts inside. It was to be hoped that each individual would find the chance to express some bit of his private experience to another individual from time to time, so as not to have passed through the universe without sounding his *peep*.

There was barking outside. I put the birthday card and book away and turned out the light, and I stepped out onto the porch. The half moon lit the sky bright gray behind the black high-voltage lines. Here came a dog, pushing its nose through the grass. Two more followed. One let out a high-pitched cry and they moved off into the woods, out of sight, though I still heard them. So did Betty, I knew.

17

THE NEXT MORNING at seven-thirty I was walking past Boo's driveway when he called to me from the carport door. He wanted the tag cut out of his T-shirt.

"I was trying to do it myself in the mirror," he said. "Which ain't easy."

He handed me a pair of manicure scissors then flipped the collar of his shirt inside out. A wooden match flew out of his shirt pocket and landed on the driveway, where a tall, lean chicken scooted up to inspect it. I picked the match up and gave it back to Boo.

"Thanks, John," he said. "Matches is very bad for chickens."

I stared at him. "We wouldn't want harm to come to a chicken," I said.

"No we wouldn't. And you don't need to mention it to Dwayne, either."

"Don't worry," I said. "Dwayne's dealings with chickens are something I never want to talk about again. And

I also don't want to know about *your* dealings with chickens."

Boo frowned. "Okay," he said slowly. "But I'm not talking about the chicken. I'm talking about the match."

"What about it?"

"I'm not supposed to be carrying it, because of my pyromania."

"You're a *pyromaniac?*"

"No, John. I'm a *person with pyromania.*"

"But you're a fireman," I said.

"I know it."

I cut the tag out and Boo rolled his shoulders and neck. "Oh, that's much better," he said. "No itchy now. Where are you headed off to on foot?"

I had hoped to slip away unnoticed, but I told him the truth. "I'm meeting Danielle McBain."

"In the woods?"

"No, in her car. We're going to the university library."

"Were you trying to slip away without me seeing?"

"Why would I want to do that?"

"You know why," Boo said. "But don't worry, I won't tell my cousin you're pursuing another girl."

"I'm *not* pursuing another girl," I said.

"Oh, excuse me. You're *visiting the library.*"

"I'm not pursuing *either* girl," I said.

"You're not?"

"No."

"Well you might want to clarify that with Dweena," Boo said. "She could have a different idea after you went on about how pretty she is."

"She told you that?"

"Of course she didn't. I was listening."

Boo dropped his chin and struck the match in a little cleft between his top front incisors. He set his shirt tag on fire and dropped it onto the gravel, where it burned and left a spot of molten goo.

I met McBain at the foot of the road as we'd planned the night before. She looked tired, and I felt the same. We rode without speaking to the campus of East Tennessee State University, in Johnson City. It was a thirty-minute drive. When we got there I had her drop me off at the library entrance, claiming I'd work more efficiently alone. It was true, but the other reason was that I didn't want McBain to see what I found until I'd had the chance to sort through it. I hadn't told her about the yellow fliers. I hoped to find something today that would send McBain off in another direction entirely.

At the library I worked quickly, starting with microfilms of the Nashville paper, piecing together some history of lottery politics in the state. I went to a Texas paper and then the *New York Times*. I flipped through bound volumes of *Fortune* from the early 1980s. In an hour and a half I'd learned enough, I was sure, to convince McBain that the story she wanted to uncover was not in Pantherville.

She showed up at the reference desk thirty minutes late, with a long brown coffee stain down the front of her blouse. Her face was even paler than usual. "What happened to you?" I said.

She held out a package of Nabs. The plastic was torn

open, and one Nab was gone. A bright crumb, annatto orange, clung at the corner of her mouth. "I've got to find something I can eat," she said weakly.

I led her out of the library and asked directions to the student union, where I bought her a plate of french fries. We went to a booth in a corner. Elbows on the table, her head dropping between her knobby shoulders, she turned a fry over feebly.

"When did you last eat?" I asked her.

"Yesterday morning, I think."

She was helpless. "You're like a baby bird in a shoe box," I said.

She moved a french fry to her mouth, bit it, and tentatively chewed.

"I'm going to tell you what you need to do," I said. "You need to go to Nashville. That's where your story is."

"What story?"

"The story of the lottery, and how it's coming to Tennessee, whether the people want it or not."

"I'm listening," she said.

"Are you? Are you able?"

She swallowed, and we both waited to see what would happen. Would the food stay down? She waved a hand in front of her face. "Start at the top," she said.

"Okay. To start with, imagine a monkey. He's in a box. Whenever he hits a certain lever, a good thing comes down a slot for him."

"What kind of a good thing?"

"A peanut, or a jellybean. The monkey learns, and whenever he's hungry or bored, he hits the lever. Now, change the system: he only gets a peanut every third time he hits the lever. What do you suppose is the result?"

"When he wants a peanut he hits the lever three times."

"Right," I said. "It's pretty much the same, and the monkey eats about as many peanuts as before. So now try a third way. The monkey hits the lever, and he gets a peanut. He hits it again, and gets nothing; he hits it twenty-five times, and still nothing comes out; and then he hits it once more and gets *five peanuts*. What happens now?"

"He eats the peanuts?"

"Yes. But he also stops sleeping, and he begins to lose weight. The reason is, now the monkey spends all day and all night banging away at the lever. Hungry or not, he can't stop himself. This is the principle of sporadic gratification."

McBain settled back and crossed her arms. She looked at me blankly.

"And it's interesting in itself," I said, "but it's especially of interest to *you* because of the use made of it by a naturalized Swedish psychologist named Tor Wennerberg, who in 1977 bought out a company called Data Branch, which had been known for building cash registers. You see, the gratification has to be sporadic not only in frequency but also in amount—a small reward sometimes, but occasionally a very big reward. The bigger it gets, the less frequent it needs to be. What Wennerberg did was to combine these behavioral principles with an early form of computer networking technology to produce the first progressive electronic lottery system. When deployed on a very large scale, with thousands or millions of players, the prize becomes correspondingly large."

"Why is this of special interest to me?" McBain said.

"Well, the problem was, when Wennerberg built this system there was no legal way to use it. Private lotteries were illegal in all fifty states. But he had the idea of selling the system to state governments. Data Branch would run it, the state would license the machines, and a percentage of the take would pay for schools or bridges. The percentage that Data Branch asked for seemed small—maybe ten cents on each dollar taken in by the lottery. That becomes a lot, though, when you get enough people playing. As of now, thirty-seven states have signed on to multistate progressive lottery games. The prizes go as high as two or three hundred million dollars.

"But all of this is well known," I said. "What's not well known is how Data Branch manages to recruit entire states as its clients. It's not a simple matter—it requires legislation, and sometimes, as in the case of Tennessee, an amendment to the constitution. How do you suppose they do this?"

"They give away pencils with the name of the company on the side," McBain said.

"They hire lobbyists who are close to the people with power in state government. Cousins or in-laws of committee chairs, former lieutenant governors—this is documented. There have been investigations, but no indictments. So far."

She nodded. She had gotten two or three of the french fries down, and her color, such as it was, was coming back. "So you think this is what's happening in Nashville," she said. "That could be kind of interesting, maybe."

"It's *very* interesting, and I *know* it is happening," I said.

"Yes. Well, the thing is, I have a suspicion about why there have not been any indictments yet, and it's because state governments, you know, can't be counted on to regulate lobbyists, or to enforce the regulations if they have them. I mean, Nashville—who knows what goes on? You'd have to have sources on the inside, which I don't. What am I going to do, just stand on the sidewalk asking people 'Are you a paid lobbyist for gambling interests?'"

"The Tennessee lobbyist for Data Branch is a man named Mike Signet," I said. "He was an up-and-comer in the House of Representatives, a leader in the upstate Republican delegation, and then he resigned a year ago. He's the one Runnels replaced."

She asked me how I knew this.

"I'm not going to tell you how I know it," I said. "All I'm telling you is that it's true, and if you will go to Nashville and look into the thing, you'll find a story that's very worthy of television. You can take this stuff." I pushed a small stack of photocopies across the table to her.

She looked at the top page, riffling the edge of the stack. "Nashville, huh? That's where they have the country music at. I think you're maybe trying to get rid of me, Tolley. Are you?"

"I sort of am," I admitted.

"You don't like the adventure I've exposed you to?"

"I'm sore," I said. "I hurt."

"What's your lobbyist's name? Mikey Christmas?"

"Mike Signet," I said.

She opened her narrow purse and brought out a small notepad. She turned some pages. *"Has forty-two-inch flat panel plasma television,"* she read.

"What?"

"Has Playstation 2. Played Smackdown and Grand Theft Auto."

"What have you got there?" I said.

"These are my reporter's notes, from my luncheon tête-à-tête with House member Ronnie."

"What is he talking about?"

"He's talking about the recreations he gets to indulge in while staying with his Nashville roommate, one *Mike Signet.*"

"His roommate? That's—"

"The blond guy from the chicken fight," she said. "That's him. Pretty good reporting, no?" She slapped the notepad shut.

"I think you must be mistaken," I said.

"And get this. How I know? Signet walks up to me outside the post office, introduces himself, and asks me for a *date.*"

"A date? I don't believe it."

"Believe it, Tolley. I stand out anywhere, but I *really* stand out in Pantherville. I mean, I'm the only female in town whose clothing doesn't have snaps on it."

"Did you have a date with him?"

"No. He's too tall, too ruddy, his neck had whiskers on it, and I did not like his manner. Under the Italian suit he's pure hills."

"How do you know his suit was Italian?"

"By briefly looking at it. Also his shoes were plasticky, though they weren't plastic. I told him maybe some other time. Then I took his friend Ronnie to lunch."

"Didn't Signet find that suspicious?"

"No. I said I was doing an interview for *Postal Worker Weekly.*"

"And he believed that?"

"I said it in an offhanded way that people find very convincing. Anyway, thanks for the suggestion, but it looks like you're wrong, and the story's in Pantherville after all. So I guess I'll be sticking around. Good effort, though. Now we'll see how these natives hold up under the cold, square eye of the camera."

"The camera has a square eye?"

"Well, no, but it has a thing on it that makes it look square. It's totally inhuman, and it turns people clear like jelly. Their chests start to jiggle and you can see their little hearts thumping inside, like pineapple chunks." She slid the plate of fries across the table. "Go to town," she said.

"What town?"

"Eat the fries, I'm saying. The rest are yours."

She flicked her eyebrows and smiled, showing her small, even teeth. Then the smile went away and she smacked her tongue. She snatched a paper napkin from the dispenser on the table and began wiping her teeth with it.

18

WE HEADED FOR PANTHERVILLE. As we were leaving Johnson City McBain asked if it was named for my "favorite president."

"I never said he was my favorite. And no, it was named for a different Johnson."

"Did you ever find your Jarvis?"

"Not so far."

"Well, I hope you will, old John. You deserve a little success."

"Thanks."

She punched me in the shoulder. Her fist was light but had a cricket-like quickness behind it.

We passed through a construction zone on Interstate 181. The lanes were narrowed with rubber cones, and the speed limit was marked fifty. McBain dug in her purse, swerving towards a highway worker in an orange vest. He stepped back, looking me in the eye as we zipped past him.

She pulled out her tiny cell phone and shook it at me. "Tolley, you and I are going over this lottery story twenty times, till it's pat as Mother Goose. Then I'm going to call Jerry Hedberg in New York and spin him a tale that will leave him wheezing. I'll have an expense account by nightfall. Just observe. And listen, I'm not going to forget you when I speak to Jerry. I'm going to mention your name. Who knows, maybe I can get you on as an assistant producer. You've got good feet, and those are few and far between."

"I have two feet, and they're the normal distance apart," I said.

"It's a figure of speech. Good feet: it means you're good at finding things out. I have good feet too, but they're a different kind of feet than yours." She glanced at me. "I'm good with people, John. You're good with reference materials."

The comment stung. She was right—I had done her work for her in the library, and while I had meant to lead her away from Dwayne Loupe, the result would be the opposite. McBain was the type to keep scratching until something bled. I wondered how Boo would take it if Dwayne went to prison.

I wondered how Dweena would take it.

"Wait just an ever-loving minute," McBain said. She straightened to an erect posture behind the wheel. "Do I *call* Jerry, or do I *go to* him?" She turned to me, staring. "They're really two distinct pitches, the phone pitch and the in-office. Oh, wow. I have to think about this."

Out the window, I watched some yellow machinery working the slope of a red clay bank. A tall, shafted

device was slamming repeatedly at a white hunk of
stone. Long lines of straw bales were staked along the
foot of the bank to slow the erosion. Then we passed an
exit with an Arby's, an Exxon, and a new two-story Bud-
getel with a sign on an eighty-foot pole. Then there was
a pasture with cows.

"You could come along, Tolley," McBain said. "You
could come to New York for the pitch."

"I just left New York," I said. "I didn't thrive there.
Also, I'm not good in meetings."

"You wouldn't speak," she said.

She dropped me off at Boo's driveway. The chickens
came running in a group. McBain powered her window
down and nodded at them significantly before driving
away.

I had no cheese puffs to share this time. The birds
moved along, scratching the ground as they went.

The chicken thought process, it struck me, was not
essentially different from the human one. I could imagine a life in which, at any moment, I might drop everything and scurry towards some tall, fuzzy object that I
had reason to believe might toss me a cheese puff. And
then, when the cheese puff did not appear, I could imagine forgetting it almost immediately, distracted by the
ground with its tasty red worms and soft leaves of clover.
That way of life was not inconceivable to me.

Boo was out, but he had left the carport door
unlocked. I went to his kitchen and returned to my pages
of Jarvises. I dialed Mr. Yancey R. Jarvis of Bristol and
went through my spiel.

"Get a life," he said.

"I have a life," I said. "This work I'm engaged in could mean the complete reevaluation of a minor American presidency."

Click.

I put my head down on the table.

I heard the carport door open and close, then footsteps.

"Are you alive?"

I sat up. It was Dweena.

She looked at me for a moment, then laid a new copy of *Nose Dog* on the table. "See you later," she said, and she left.

I went outside. Her Wagoneer was in the driveway, clicking softly. I walked to the far end of the house and climbed the pressure-treated steps to her apartment. There were healthy potted plants on the landing. I knocked. She opened the door, holding a banana, and aimed her big brown-irised eyes at me.

I asked her if she knew anything about some flyers against the lottery that had been mailed, or not mailed.

"Flyers?" She took a bite.

"You know, mailers. Broadsides. Have you seen any? Do you know what I'm talking about?"

"I see a lot of flyers," she said. "I put them in the mailboxes."

She spoke calmly. The question seemed to surprise her a little, but there was no note of defensiveness. Whatever was going on with the nondelivery of these flyers, she had nothing to do with it, I was certain.

"I want to ask you to forgive whatever strange or rude things I may have said to you when I was partly unconscious in Nashville," I said. "There's a gap in my memory."

"If there's a gap then you don't know what I said, either."

"That is true."

"Well, just forget about it," she said. "I'm not vain."

I knew very well she wasn't vain.

"Excuse me while I brush my teeth," she said.

She left me with the door standing open. I looked inside. There was a dim, small living room with one metal bookcase, waist-high, holding paperbacks, and a board on the floor with a jigsaw puzzle on it, almost finished. Because of the angle I couldn't make out what the picture was.

When Dweena returned she was wearing a green ball cap. She came outside and shut the door. "Have you found your Jarvis yet?" she said.

"No. I guess you heard about that project from Boo."

"I heard at the post office. Lionel Jarvis told me all of his people are getting calls."

I followed her down the stairs and across the yard. "It's odd that he mentioned it," I said.

"Not really. He knows you live here."

"He does?"

"Everybody does," she said.

"How?"

She got into the Wagoneer—passenger side—and shut the door. "This isn't New York," she said. "There's not that much to pay attention to. Also Dwayne's been bragging on you."

"He has?"

"Yes. 'My nephew's historian friend.' He likes you."

"Why?"

"Because of Boo," she said.

"I don't get it."

She frowned. "Have you noticed that Boo doesn't have a lot of friends?"

I had noticed it. I also remembered what Dweena had told me about her uncle looking out for Boo.

"Dwayne seems to trust you for some reason," she said somberly.

"Hold on," I said. "If everybody knows everything around here, why doesn't somebody just direct me to Edna Jarvis?"

"We don't know of any such Jarvis," she said.

"Well there was one. Her name is engraved in brass at the Johnson museum."

"Brownie's name is engraved in brass on her collar."

"Do you know any Johnson descendants?"

"I know dozens of Johnsons," she said. "It's a common surname."

"Tell me about it."

"Sometimes they even marry each other, and then you've got Johnson Johnsons."

I told her I thought it unlikely that a woman marrying into that situation would continue to use both Johnsons in her name.

"A woman on my route does," Dweena said.

"She must come from an unusually proud line of Johnsons. Is her first name Johnson too?"

"No, it's Edna."

"Edna?" I pondered on this for a few parts of a second. "Well why didn't you tell me?"

"Tell you what?"

"This could easily be my Edna Johnson Jarvis! Mr. Johnson might be her second husband—I mean her third! How old is she?"

"I don't know. I've never seen her. I know she gets social security."

"Intriguing! Do you think there's a chance she's related to President Johnson?"

"With her being a Johnson Johnson, I guess there's a better than average chance."

I ran around the front of the Wagoneer and got in on the driver's side. "Take me there," I said.

"I've got my mail to deliver," Dweena said.

"You said she's on your route, correct? You can make the stops as we go."

She put her left leg across the hump and cranked the Wagoneer. I squeezed against the driver's-side door. She backed us out smoothly.

"Wait," I said. "Can I go up to the knob first to get my tweed jacket?"

She blinked at me slowly, then put the Wagoneer in reverse and backed it up the hill.

19

"MRS. JOHNSON WONDER WHEN you will visit," the nurse said.

"I beg your pardon?"

"Yard boy tell me someone asking for Andrew Johnson great grand-daughter. We wonder why you never come here."

"Yard boy?"

"Yard boy. Mow yard."

I was standing at the entrance to a rather grand brick house set well back from the road, speaking to an Asian woman who had identified herself as Mrs. Johnson's nurse. "I had the wrong name," I said. "I was looking for a Mrs. Jarvis."

The nurse smiled. "Please, we never mention Jarvis," she said. "This was very unhappy short marriage. Mrs. Johnson never want to be remind."

"I'm sorry. I won't bring it up," I said.

"Mr. Jarvis give special slippers away to museum.

They divorce." The nurse stepped back and motioned me into the foyer.

"I see. Then she married Mr. Johnson," I said.

"No. Then she marry Hostetler. Move to Indiana. Bad, bad move."

"She didn't like Indiana?"

"I can no understand what any people say there. Strange, uh, dialect. Then she marry Johnson. Johnson die."

"I wonder if I might speak with Mrs. Johnson?"

"You stand here. I go see." The nurse left.

On the wall beside a hall tree hung a gilt-framed portrait: a stern, sad-seeming Andrew Johnson towards the end of his life, dressed in full Masonic regalia.

"Come, come!" the nurse called from the next room. She reappeared, smiling. "Mrs. Johnson see you."

I followed her into a large, formal living room.

"Mrs. Johnson, this Mr. Tolley," the nurse said.

From her seat in the middle of a long sofa, Mrs. Johnson held out both arms to me.

I was unsure what to do. I held out my hand, though I was still several steps across the room from her.

The nurse whispered, "She like to hug you. Do it."

I approached the elderly woman. I guessed she was in her eighties. She would have been rather tall, had she been standing. Her hair was a sandy color, very neatly arranged, and she wore a green dress and gold earrings. I leaned down and patted her sleeves. She grabbed my left elbow with a plierslike grip and shook it, then let it go.

"Mrs. Johnson, I can't tell you how glad I am to be meeting you. I've come to do research on your great-grandfather the president," I said. "You are the great-granddaughter of Andrew Johnson, aren't you?"

"Yes, yes," she said. Her voice was hoarse, and she cleared her throat loudly.

"Particularly I am eager to learn about your relative Mr. Robert Stovall. He was the nephew of your grandmother. Do you have any knowledge of him?"

She raised a hand to her lips, thoughtfully. "Oh yes," she said, blinking.

The blood was thrumming against my eardrums. There was a small tape recorder in the pocket of my Osim Lowe jacket, and I brought it out and asked Mrs. Johnson's permission to use it.

"Yes," she said. She smiled at me.

I jumped back several inches. Mrs. Johnson's teeth were bright red.

I turned to find the nurse, but she was gone. I ran back to the foyer and called for her. She came running, holding a doughnut. "What what what?" she said.

"Mrs. Johnson needs your help immediately! Look at her mouth!" I pointed.

Mrs. Johnson, still sitting up on the sofa, grinned at the nurse.

"Oh, Mrs. Johnson, why did you do that?" the nurse said. She went to Mrs. Johnson and, kneeling in front of her, grabbed her chin dexterously, using the hand that also held the doughnut. With her other hand she pulled a tissue from a pocket and began wiping roughly at Mrs. Johnson's teeth. "Where you find lipstick? I can't keep it hide from you. You a handful, Mrs. Johnson."

Mrs. Johnson sat patiently, head up, while her teeth were cleaned. I stared without thinking until it occurred to me to turn my back.

Then the nurse walked past me. "She okay," the nurse said.

I gave myself a moment to settle. Then I went to the point. "I need to know everything you can tell me about Robert Stovall, Mrs. Johnson. Who keep in touch with him? I mean, who *kept* in touch with him?"

Mrs. Johnson frowned, as though thinking. "Yes," she said.

I waited for more, but none came. "Do you know where I might find any of this information, Mrs. Johnson?"

"Yes," she said.

"Will you tell me?"

"Yes."

"You're not understanding my questions, are you?"

"Yes," she said. "Yes."

She covered her mouth and coughed.

I sat down in a chintz-covered wingback chair. On the coffee table in front of Mrs. Johnson there was a wooden coaster set and nothing else. There were five tall windows in the wall behind her. Outside, the day was bright.

"Johnson was not one of our better presidents," I said.

Mrs. Johnson looked at me with a vague expression on her face. She touched her forehead.

"Nor was he one of the very worst," I said. "The truth is, he was somewhat below average."

Using both hands, Mrs. Johnson lifted her wig off and set it on the sofa next to her.

I got up. "Excuse me, please," I said.

"Yes."

I wandered back into the house and found the nurse in the kitchen, picking through a box of Krispy Kreme doughnuts. "Mrs. Johnson doesn't say anything but 'Yes,'" I said.

"Mm." The nurse licked her finger. "She senile!"

"I thought you said she was eager to see me!"

"She like anybody visit! She get bored like me."

"I've got to go," I said. "I'll let myself out."

"Bye."

I pointed at a door. "Is that the back way?"

"You don't go that way. You go front door."

"Mrs. Johnson has removed her hairpiece," I said. "I don't know what else she may have removed."

"You be okay. Go." She pointed towards the front.

I found my way back to the foyer and slipped past the living room entry with my head down. I grabbed the doorknob. I felt small, though.

I went back to the living room. Mrs. Johnson was on the sofa pretty much as I had left her. I offered my hand, which she took, and I thanked her for her time. She nodded, staring past me, and then I left.

20

THIS DISAPPOINTMENT WAS a rather intense one.

A cracked concrete walkway led straight down the yard to a set of steps that stopped at the edge of a county road. Only now did it occur to me that I didn't have a ride. I started walking.

Here was my thought. Where the effort is noble, there is no shame in failure. *But where the effort was stupid to begin with,* some shame is appropriate.

What had ever led me to believe that I could find, in Tennessee or anywhere, a book of clippings that Martha Johnson Patterson had caused to be lost over one hundred years before?

The explanation was this. In the cool, quiet sanctuary of a New York City Public Library reading room, I had formed an idea about Tennessee. In my imagination its hills, trees, and people were constructed of brightly colored fiberglass resin, and three-inch speakers were hidden here and there to play the story of Tennessee when a button was pressed.

Clearly, something was wrong with me—something basic. There was a screwiness, deep down. It seemed I had never had any chance of not failing.

I talked to myself, as I walked, in the most maudlin and pathetic tone. My feet felt mealy inside the hard wing tips. Sweat gathered in my eyebrows and armpits, and then it broke in streams down the sides of my chest. In a fit of frustration I whipped off the Osim Lowe jacket and flung it into some blackberries. I walked away, abandoning it.

My tape recorder was in the pocket, and also a Parker Jotter. Well, I abandon them too, I thought. Then I got to wondering what else might be in the pockets and I went back like the tame thing I was and extracted my jacket from the stickers, sustaining the usual scratches to my hands and face that I get anytime I go near a blackberry plant.

Something clicked. It was the tape running out on my tape recorder. The thing had been recording this whole time, so now I had the pleasure of listening to the entire humiliating episode over again, from my yelp at the sight of Mrs. Johnson's grisly smile to the climactic flinging of the blazer and its retrieval, accompanied by modest *ouch*es.

I walked a long time, and then a man in a truck gave me a ride to Mark's Repair. There was my Duster, parked in a corner of the red-dirt lot, still dead, and still yellow as corn. I went to the small office with its large picture window where Mark and an employee were eating chili from Styrofoam bowls at the desk. "I'm ready to have that work done on the Duster," I said. I would put it on Zimmer's Visa.

Mark set his spoon down and chewed for several seconds silently before asking me to remind him who I was.

"I'm the one who brought the Duster," I said. "You told me you could fix it for four hundred dollars."

"I said I could put a water pump on it for four hundred dollars," he said. "It also needs tires."

"It needs a single tire," I said.

"I don't normally sell singles," Mark said. "That's like selling a shoe."

The employee had stopped eating too, now, and looked at me.

"I have always bought my tires one at a time," I said.

"They wouldn't blow so bad if you'd keep air in them," Mark said.

I considered. "For a thousand dollars I'll sell you the car."

Mark made a face as though I had jabbed him with a pencil. He adjusted himself in his chair. "I could give you three hundred dollars," he said.

"I'd take a thousand for it. That's barely half what I paid for the car."

"I can't help what you paid," Mark said. "I see a car that doesn't run."

"Eight hundred," I said.

"I'll give you three hundred and fifty dollars," Mark said. "Bring the title and we'll settle up."

I acquiesced. I was hungry. I went to the Maisy Restaurant and was slinking towards a table in the rear of the nonsmoking section when I spotted the lead-gray curls of Dwayne Loupe. I turned quickly to leave, hoping he had not seen me.

"Young John," he called to my back. "Come join us."

I turned around again to look at him. He sat alone.

"I'm having lunch with all my friends," he said.

"Where are they?"

The waitress walked up from behind me. "That's the joke, Johnny," she said. She stopped beside Loupe and faced me with her weight on one leg.

I asked her how she knew my name.

"Is your name Johnny? I was just calling you that."

"Come join us," Loupe said again.

I sat down with him. The waitress asked if I wanted a menu.

"Special's good," Loupe said.

"That'll be fine."

"Chicken or meat loaf?" the waitress asked me.

"Chicken."

"Green beans, pinto beans, creamed potatoes, coleslaw, turnip greens, apple fritter, fried eggplant, or corn? You get two."

"Creamed potatoes," I said. "A double order."

"Cornbread or roll?"

"Get the roll," Loupe said.

I nodded.

"And what to drink?"

"Water."

"Thank you," she said, and she left.

"You look sad, John," Loupe said.

"I've been walking."

"That's nothing to be sad about. A long June walk, culminating in a great big late lunch at the Maisy." He stared at me, drumming his car-hood fingernails on the dull, hard surface of the table. "You like it here, don't you?"

"I haven't done so well here," I said.

"I bet some of our ways strike you as backward, coming from other states and countries as you do."

"Ways strike me as backward everywhere," I said.

"It's a big world with many cultures in it, as you know."

I told him yes, I did know that.

"And yet you don't show respect for *my* culture," Loupe said.

"I don't know what you mean."

Loupe glanced into spaces around the room as though searching for words. "John," he said, "I know a boy who sat up crying half of last night."

I asked why the boy was crying.

"I think you know why," Loupe said.

"No, I don't."

"He was crying because someone sprayed pepper in his face," Loupe said. "Would you know about that?"

I eased back from the table a bit. I said nothing.

"And why did this boy get sprayed?" Loupe said. "Was he out making trouble? Spray-painting highway underpasses? Drinking alcohol, participating in gangs? No.

This boy was at home, enjoying a pastime that he learned from his father and grandfather. Not hurting a soul, John—just being a normal, enthusiastic East Tennessee boy, until someone invaded his barn space."

The waitress brought my water and I quickly drank half the glass. "Let me be direct," I said. "First of all, I don't know that I have any idea what you're referring to."

"Of course you don't," Loupe said. "Neither one of us does. I'm not sure we're even here."

"But it seems to me," I went on, "surely something provoked the spraying. Maybe this boy grabbed someone and frightened her or him."

"That doesn't explain what the person was doing outside the boy's barn."

"Exploring, maybe," I said. "Possibly the person was lost."

Loupe gave a long, unhappy frown. He shifted in his chair and pulled out his wallet, which he opened on the table and began organizing. It was jammed with business cards and folded slips of paper with printing or writing on them. The leather was partly worn through at the crease. It was the wallet of a rather disorganized rural American man of affairs.

While watching Dwayne Loupe engaged in this business I was reminded that I had no cash with me. I had spent all I was carrying on McBain's fries. I flagged down the waitress to cancel my order, but Loupe said he would pay.

"I'd rather you not," I said.

"Oh, please," Loupe said. "You're making me feel bad."

He sighed and went back to sorting the contents of his billfold. He pulled out a torn-off slip. "I have no idea whose phone number this is," he said. "Until I remember, I can't throw it away."

"Mr. Loupe, I've got to tell you something," I said.

"Call me Dwayne."

"The person we're talking about—the one who sprayed the boy—this person knows some things about you."

"About me?"

"About you and Mike Signet," I said, lowering my voice. "About you, Mike Signet, Ronnie, and the lottery, and Data Branch."

Dwayne Loupe looked away quickly, then looked back at me. He squinted.

"She's a journalist," I said. "She'll learn more—she's tenacious. I tried to steer her away from you."

"You tried to *steer* her?"

Our food came. Loupe returned the little stacks of cards and slips to his wallet and put it away.

"I tried to steer her towards Nashville and away from Pantherville," I said.

"Why?"

"I was trying to help you," I said.

"You were trying to help me," Loupe repeated. He contemplated that, and then he took a one-ounce plastic bottle from his shirt pocket and squeezed a dab of clear gel into his palm. He rubbed his hands together, then held the bottle out. "Would you like to sanitize before we eat?"

"Yes, please," I said.

He squirted a drop into my hand, and then we ate.

"You can't help me, John," Loupe said. "You don't know the situation, and even if you did, you're just not a person who could ever possibly help me in this matter."

"My sense of ethics does make it difficult," I said.

"Oh. Well, that too, but that's not what I meant. You're an intelligent person, John, but you have what I would call some blind spots."

"Doesn't everyone?"

"Yes. But everyone doesn't have *your* blind spots."

Tired of talking in circles, I asked him directly whether Mike Signet had offered him a bribe to dump those flyers.

The question clearly surprised him. Loupe stopped chewing briefly, and then he sat back and swallowed and wiped his mouth with a napkin. After some time, he nodded yes.

"What's more, I took it," Loupe said. "It was a large amount. I tell you this to give you an idea of the seriousness of this business. You need to stay clear of it."

I set down my fork and looked around me. The waitress had gone in back, and the only other person around was across the room, getting out of his chair. He laid some dollars on the table and left.

"I can't believe what I'm hearing," I said. My eyes landed on the United States Postal Service insignia on his shirt pocket. I pointed my finger at it.

He brushed at his shirt with a napkin, until he saw what I meant. He nodded. "I know, it's discouraging," he said. "People have a certain idea about the integrity of a postmaster. You have to take my word that the situation is highly complex. Maybe if you stick around you'll understand it someday, though not soon."

"Does Dweena know?"

"Of course not." Possibly there was a faint hint of shame at the mention of his niece, but Loupe stifled it quickly. "Dweena would have nothing to do with Mike Signet or any of this. You wouldn't even find her speaking to him."

I told him I trusted that Dweena would have better sense than to involve herself in this kind of affair, but I did not think it would be obvious at all to someone who didn't know her. "You had her driving Runnels to Nashville," I said.

"We help each other out," Loupe said.

"But you make her look guilty. And here's another problem I have with you," I said. "You fight chickens, and that's wrong."

"Well, you caused a chicken to be killed, fried, and laid on a plate," Loupe said.

"This is my lunch."

"And this is mine," Loupe said. He ate a bite of meat-loaf emphatically.

"Chicken fighting is a primitive blood sport," I said.

"Have you ever observed a rooster closely, town boy?"

"Somewhat closely."

"If you spend some time with them you'll see that they are rather rudimentary in their motives. It's mainly all to do with sex and eating, for them. The fighting is a by-product of the sex."

"I don't see how that follows."

"Of course you do. Have you never been unhappy with another male because of a female?"

"This is ridiculous," I said.

"Why does a rooster have spurs?"

"To fight in the wild," I said. "But you strap metal blades to their legs."

"Those are called gaffs, John. The bird likes wearing those. They make him feel cocky. *Cocky*—you see? It's a trait we don't admire in humans, but we expect it from roosters."

"And there's also nothing natural about dropping two birds in a pit together," I said. "There's a fence around the pit! If the birds were fighting in nature, one of them could run away!"

"True," Loupe said. "The pit is our contribution."

"That disgusts me," I said.

"And yet this is all right," he said, indicating my plate. Between the mounds of creamed potatoes were three long strips of batter-fried breast meat.

"I need to eat," I said.

I ate some bites of chicken, though it was harder to enjoy now.

Loupe said, "Consider this, young John. The birds I raise grow up in fresh air, are fed on beef strips and tobacco juice, are trained and exercised and given vitamins and live insects and greens, and get to act out their most basic primal urges in a dirt hole with men cheering. They either die fairly quick or get put to stud. It's a glorious life for them."

"Chickens don't aspire to glory," I said.

"Right there is where you're wrong. A male chicken aspires to glory every day of his life. He wakes up hollering, struts and barks all day, and goes to bed hollering at night. Glory is exactly what he aspires to. He may not be the brightest creature on earth."

I gave up. I had no rebuttal.

Loupe said, "You keep looking at that fritter, John. Why don't you eat it?"

"I'm not looking at it," I said.

"Eat the fritter, son."

Conflicted, I took Loupe's fritter and ate it. It was good.

"Does Boo fight chickens too?" I said.

"No, no. He has no interest in that activity. His birds are some of my culls that should've been mashed on the head, but he wouldn't let me."

That was the end of lunch. I told Dwayne Loupe I would come by the post office later in the day, or the next day, to pay him back for my meal.

"You buy me lunch one day," he said.

Loupe was tenacious, I thought. What made him so sure I wouldn't write a letter to the U.S. Postal Inspection Service about him? I told him there would be no opportunity for us to have lunch again, because I intended to leave Tennessee as soon as possible.

"Going back to New York City?" he said.

"Probably not." When McBain learned that I had tipped off Dwayne Loupe, her offer to make me an assistant producer, whatever that was, would evaporate. I might also wind up with fingernail marks to go with my blackberry scratches. "It looks like I'll be heading back to Ohio," I said. Then I had another thought. "If you would, please pass this along to that boy." I brought the captured Barlow from my pocket and laid it on the table. Loupe frowned at it and nodded.

We sat awhile in silence. Loupe looked past me, watching something. "That's why they call it the Maisy," he said.

"Why?"

"Because you *may see* someone you don't want to see."

"Frankly, you were the last person I wanted to run into," I said.

"And that man who just walked in didn't want to see you."

"Impossible," I said. "I'm totally harmless and bland."

"Who owes you money?"

"No one, unfortunately."

"I'm afraid the only possibility left is that he doesn't like you."

I turned to look.

"He's gone now," Loupe said.

"What did he look like?"

"Hungry."

"How does a person look hungry?"

"I don't know. He was an enormous fat man wearing sandals."

21

I RAN OUT THE FRONT in time to catch Dr. Luke Van
Brun in the parking lot with his fist in his front
pocket. His jeans were tighter than they ought to have
been, and the key ring which he now produced with a
final tug had too many keys on it. The delay had pre-
vented his escape. "Damn this key ring and these jean
pants," he said.

I stopped square in front of him. "Why are you here?"
I said. I glanced inside his brown Volvo, where something
very interesting caught my eye.

"Well I'm seen, so I may as well eat," Van Brun said.
"Is this place any good? It looks like the sort of place that
might be better than it looks."

He started back to the Maisy, and I followed him. We
passed Dwayne Loupe on his way out. "Have a pleasant
rest of the day, John," Loupe said.

Van Brun went to a table and sat.

"Why are you here?" I asked him again.

The waitress spoke up beside me. "To eat, I hope," she said.

She handed him a menu. He glanced at it, then set it aside. He wanted her to *tell* him about the food, he said. "What's the dish everyone's talking about?" He asked how each item was prepared. What puzzled me was that the waitress answered all of his questions cheerfully and with no sign of impatience. I won't record the whole exchange but will simply state the lesson I took, which is that everyone is indeed different, not only in his own behavior but in the effect he has on others. Van Brun was an outstanding example of this.

I sat down. When the waitress left, I asked Van Brun why he had tried to avoid me.

"I wasn't trying to avoid you," he said. "I had forgotten something in my car."

"What did you forget?"

"I left the air conditioner running," he said.

"That's impossible. The keys were in your pocket."

"It's unlikely, but it's not impossible."

"You're lying," I said. My voice was small and choked-sounding. "You saw me here and left. I noticed you have some Krispy Kreme napkins on the seat."

"So?"

"Did you have doughnuts this morning?"

He looked at me for a long moment, then pursed his lips, then covered his mouth with his hand. "Yes. I made a doughnut run," he said.

"I know someone else who had doughnuts today of the same brand," I said. "I wonder if there's a connection."

Tremors broke out across his large face, and finally he could not hold back. The tittering turned to open laughter at my expense.

"I don't see what's so funny," I said. "You beat me to Mrs. Johnson by a few hours at most."

"By a few minutes," Van Brun said. "I just now left."

"Were you there when I was there?"

"Yes." He stopped laughing. "I was hiding in the pantry."

"You are undignified," I said. "A man like you has no place on the faculty of a Vanderbilt University."

"You can relax," he said, wide-eyed. "You'll be glad to know I am no longer employed by that venerable institution. They have fired my ass."

The waitress came with a full tray of food. Unable to decide between the specials, he had ordered both. He apologized to the waitress, saying, "Excuse my rough language, young lady. Your step is so light, I didn't hear your approach."

The waitress was no younger than he, and surely knew his fawning flattery for what it was. She laid out the two big plates and the many small dishes of side orders and left.

"I thought you were beginning a sabbatical," I said.

He winced. "That's a half-truth I have been using to spare myself embarrassment. The actual terms of separation I am not at liberty to disclose, and neither is the administration, which leaves me free to invent when I am speaking with people I expect never to see again." He forked a chunk of meatloaf into his large and frightening mouth and crushed it, then hummed to himself and then abruptly stopped humming and shook his head. He seemed to consider what to do next, and then he reluctantly swallowed. He moved the plates so that the chicken special was in front of him.

I asked him was he drunk.

"Would I were," he said. His lower eyelids drooped. "I will be soon. But no, that's not why they fired me."

"Are you some kind of deviant?"

He raised his hand and held it in front of his mouth to speak while he chewed. "That's crude language, Mr. Tolley," he said.

"Tell me what happened."

"There was a complaint, filed by a young woman," he said. "Then a lawsuit."

"A student of yours?"

"A former student, yes."

"And were you guilty?"

"I did what she said I did. Whether my career should be artificially brought to a close, so near to what would have been its natural end—well, that is less easy to say. Possibly it should. Possibly it should have been ended a long time ago, not because of this but for more basic reasons. That's the aggravation, you see. I'm being canned, but not for the reason I *ought* to be canned."

"What did you do to her?"

He dabbed at his mouth with a napkin. "It's more interesting for you to guess," he said.

"You offered her a grade in return for sexual favors," I said.

He smiled. "In this case that would have been point-
less. She was an excellent student."

"You lowered her grade because she denied sexual
favors?"

"Much as I hate to put an end to your speculations,
which are revealing very much about you, I will tell you
the truth. I lifted part of a paper from her."

"You *plagiarized?*"

"'Plagiarized.' I don't like that term. It was a combination of oversight, fatigue, lack of time, lack of dili-
gence, and honest error. I had read the essay in question,
and I later got her ideas mixed up with my own. Very
likely they were ideas which I myself had suggested to
her in seminar."

"Is that a firing offense?"

"I had some of her language mixed up with mine as
well."

I considered and admitted that I could see how that
might happen. "Especially if one has a keen ear for the
cadences of prose," I said. "A phrase can stick in one's
memory, apart from the source of that phrase."

Van Brun gave me a long, unpleasant look.

"Okay, I'm lying again," he said. "I copied several
pages out of her master's thesis. I was in a rush."

He shrank a little in his chair. I said nothing.

"I thought no one would know. Nobody reads these
damned journals. *Proceedings of the Early Southwest Historical Society.* Come on, brother. What are the chances?
This is a journal edited by a crony of mine. Hell, it was a
book review, not even an essay. A tiny review in eight-

point type, strictly back pages. It's the sort of thing you do
to say you're publishing. Who knew she would read it?
Who knew anyone would?"

I was aghast.

Van Brun set his fork down. He raised both shiny,
mitt-like hands, and his gaze rose towards the ceiling. He
pushed his chair back from the table. He patted his shirt
pocket, then he tapped at his mouth with two fingers. He
took a lighter from his pocket and lit it, then extin-
guished it and fumbled with it in his fingers before putting it away again. He sat up straight and pivoted
towards the waitress, who was just outside his field of
vision, and he said, "May I have a cup of coffee, dear?"

"You may," came the answer.

"There are so many ways to booger up one's life," he
said quietly.

"What have you come here for?" I asked him.

"Obviously, it has something to do with your Johnson
lead."

"You deprecated my lead when I described it to you."

"Yes, I did."

"And yet, here you come now to follow up on it."

"Funny, ain't it?"

"I would have preferred, as a courtesy, for you simply
to have given me Mrs. Johnson's current name to begin
with. If you had told me how to reach her I would have
gladly—I would have *proudly*, Dr. Van Brun—shared
the results with you. I take it you had not spoken with
Edna Johnson in recent years."

"No, no. I renewed our acquaintance after you and I spoke."

"If you'd wanted, you might have come with me to interview her. We might have worked together. This is a very low business—a person of your former stature, stooping to tactics like this. Hiding in a pantry. Any young researcher would have been honored to provide you with assistance, but instead you take their work and share none of the credit. I ask you why—rhetorically, without wanting to hear your answer, which could only be meaningless. At any rate, you now know you have come five hours for nothing. You've wasted a day, which is far less than I've wasted. If you had given me the name when I was in Nashville, I could have saved you the trouble of driving here just to find that Edna Johnson is nonverbal."

"Edna is not nonverbal," Van Brun said.

"Correct. She can say one word."

"No." He laughed, then stopped himself. "She knows a great many words, my friend. She was pretending."

"What? Why?"

"Because she's a card, Tolley. We saw you trudging up that walk like a priest in a high church wedding, and I told her who you were, and so forth—I guess I said a few things that she interpreted a certain way, and she decided to have some cruel fun. The lipstick was Dorothea's idea."

"Dorothea?"

"The nurse. It was funny, but the wig was too much. That crossed a line. When you watch Edna pull a stunt

like that, you can see why she's been married so darned
many times. What *won't* she do? She proposed to me
once, you know. Well, twice, now."

"I don't believe this," I said.

"It's a relationship I worked hard to cultivate," Van
Brun said. "I never did anything improper—I mean,
well, *obviously*, the woman is much older than I. She
always has been."

He laughed.

"But in this kind of work," he went on, "one's rela-
tions with the family are everything. You can spend your
hours in the library, fine—but all that stuff has been
combed through already. And if you want to get what the
family has, you have to win their trust. Heirs of minor
presidents can be amazingly protective."

"What did you tell her, to turn her against me?"

"Well, I simply described your essay, which I finally
got around to reading the other day. In particular your
little note about Johnson's alleged racism."

"'Alleged'? He was obviously racist!"

"The word *racism* did not exist before 1936," Van
Brun said.

"He was a bigot, then!"

"Well, certainly he was a *bigot*. But that's beside the
point. Can you assure me, Mr. Tolley, as a point of honor,
that if Mrs. Johnson provided you with information leading to the recovery of the missing Johnson scrapbook,
you would report the contents of that scrapbook fully
and accurately, for the sake of complete disclosure in the
historical record?"

"Absolutely yes," I said.

"There you go. That is not what Edna Johnson wants."

"What does she want?"

"She wants her great-grandfather's name to be protected. There are obviously some unflattering discoveries to be made in that scrapbook, Tolley. Worse than unflattering."

"Did she know about the book?"

"Her uncle had spoken of it, she now claims. She made no mention of it thirty years ago, for which I could wring her frail neck. But she says no one knew whether to believe him. He was one of these family oddballs. Kept goats in the house, et cetera. Had conversation with goats. Franciscan mania. The interesting thing: she says he was a pack rat."

"He was?"

"A compulsive saver. You couldn't make him throw anything out. His little log cabin was packed to the ceiling with newspapers and folded flour sacks."

"What cabin? Where was it?"

"Settle, please," Van Brun said. "You're putting me on edge."

I sat back.

The waitress brought Van Brun's coffee. She asked him if something was wrong with his food.

"It's lovely, thanks, but I can't eat it now," he said.

"Do you want me to box it up for you, hon?"

"No thank you. I'm traveling."

She carried an armload of plates away.

"Where is the cabin?" I said.

"The site is evidently not far off," Van Brun said. "Robert Stovall spent the last of his days there, alone and intestate. When he died, the Pattersons sold the land to a farmer named Kronmiller."

"What did Kronmiller do with the cabin?"

"According to Edna, he boarded it up so his cows wouldn't fall through the floor."

"Does she think the book might be there?"

"She says it could be."

He sipped his coffee.

"Tell me where," I said.

He inserted an index finger in his shirt pocket and brought out a yellow sticky note. The writing was illegible.

"I can't read that," I said.

He squinted at it. *"The Kronmiller farm."*

"Where is the Kronmiller farm?"

"That I don't know."

"Didn't you ask Mrs. Johnson?"

"Yes, of course."

"Well?"

"I say she's not nonverbal, and she isn't," Van Brun said, "but she is a touch vague with directions. More than a touch."

"Does the cabin exist, or not?"

"All one can do is look," Van Brun said.

At that, he looked away from me. Something else had caught his attention.

From behind me I heard a loud female voice. *"Tolley.*

Where have you been?" It was Danielle McBain. Her
clear enunciation and spot-on vowels were not to be mistaken for anyone else's in this neighborhood. She stopped
at our table and stared at Van Brun. "I was looking for
you," she said.

"For me?" Van Brun said.

"No, him," McBain said. She tipped her head at me.

"How did you find me?" I said.

"I searched all of Pantherville. It took me four minutes."

Van Brun heaved himself upwards several inches. "I
am Luke Van Brun," he said.

"Danielle McBain," she said.

"You are not from here, Ms. McBain," Van Brun said.

"Of course I'm not. I've come from New York and I'm
covering a breaking story for a nationally broadcast cable
news program," she said. "I can't share the details, but it
involves allegations of official corruption, bribery, rack-
eteering, cruelty to animals, money laundry, postal fraud,
and federal and state tax evasion." She glanced at me. "I
just got off the *horn* with my producer, Tolley, and
there's a few things he wants me to triple-check before
he'll send a crew down by commercial jet."

"I thought you were going to New York for the pitch,"
I said.

"I pitched it over the phone," she said. "Uh, the
organization I'm with"—she was addressing Van Brun
again now—"is extremely scrupulous when it comes to
documenting facts. As a journalist I find it burdensome
but also necessary, I'm afraid." She spotted a fritter on its
own small plate, which the waitress had not had room for

on her arm. McBain said, "What is that, some kind of a fried pie?"

"That is exactly what it is," Van Brun said.

She sniffed. "Possibly I could eat one if it were fried quickly in a very hot, clean peanut oil, but I wouldn't risk it here. I am slightly ravenous."

"I had doughnuts earlier," Van Brun said. "Incidentally, I am a historian. Mr. Tolley has just now caught me trying to steal his very rare Andrew Johnson lead."

"John has a rare Johnson lead?" She turned to me with an expression of hilarious skepticism.

"Oh yes," Van Brun said. "He could easily remake the whole field of Johnson studies. Unfortunately, if he does it will matter but little, since nobody gives a gray rat's ass about Andrew Johnson."

"That's not true," I said.

"Believe me, I know," Van Brun said. "I authored a Johnson biography, and the lack of response was appalling." He said to McBain, "Won't you sit down?"

She squinted at the free chair next to him. She didn't answer but said to me, "So John, I pitched the story, and New York is not ready yet."

"New York," Van Brun said. "It has been too long."

"They want me to broaden the proof. I told them we saw the guy strangle a chicken, but that didn't excite."

"It's hard to excite the already excited," Van Brun said. "You're talking about a city that is a cultural and financial capital of the world, with nine or more ethnic cuisines per block, all-night bookshops and art cinema, *the theater*, and the greatest, most vast market for hand-cobbled shoes on the continent. All I can wear now are these mail-order sandals," he said, raising his foot to show us. "These feet of mine can't tolerate a factory shoe."

From the front of the restaurant, Boo walked in. The waitress waved him over and they crossed the floor in a moving huddle. They went into the kitchen.

"I was mugged for a Sunday *Times*," McBain said.

"It happens," Van Brun said without surprise.

"I had bought my paper and this person steps up and says, 'Give me your paper.' 'Buy your own,' I said. He says, 'No. I want that one. You buy another.' So I said, 'Are you planning to force me? Are you telling me this is a *mugging*?' And he says, 'Yes, this is a mugging! I am mugging you for your paper!' So, what am I going to do? Take a black eye? I gave him the paper! Then I had to walk *back* to the newsstand to get another one, and now I don't have the money for a coffee."

"It is one of the world's great cities," Van Brun said.

"It exhausts me," McBain said.

"I could never live there," Van Brun said.

"Not everyone can."

"Well, it would be absurd for everyone to live in one city. There wouldn't be room. But what I am saying is that I, personally, could never leave the South."

McBain sat down in the chair next to me and pulled the fritter close to look at it. She tilted the plate to change the angle at which the light hit the crust.

"The South is my home and must remain so," Van Brun said. "My grand old bankrupted and glorious section. Have you visited Nashville?" he asked her.

She ignored him, studying the fritter. She looked up for the waitress.

"If East Tennessee is as far as you've come, you've not entered the proper South," he said. "There was never a plantation culture in the upstate. Do you know why?"

McBain looked thoughtful. She cocked her head to one side, and the rudderlike nose showed its interesting curve, which was slight and only visible from a certain narrow angle.

"Geography is the answer," Van Brun said, flashing a grin that was both condescending and brown. He spread his arms with a double flourish.

Vanderbilt was rid of Van Brun, but he carried the air of academe with him like a cloudy train. His eyebrows, great long sloppy swipes of excessive articulateness, quivered as though they would swirl. The eyebrows were too expressive. Nobody's thoughts are so subtle or fine as to require that degree of qualification. His sensuous mouth was giving me the willies.

McBain looked at me and said, "I don't buy that Old South crap."

I approved of her skepticism. But to my surprise, so did Van Brun!

He pursed his lips and let the brows roll rakishly. "Tolley, she's formidable," he said. "New Yorkers almost always buy the Old South crap."

McBain sat up straight. "I'm not buying anybody's crap," she said. "I've got my crap detector on."

Van Brun hummed, deeply satisfied now.

22

McBAIN ASKED THE WAITRESS, who was rolling up silverware at another table, "What kind of potato do you have?"

"Regular old potatoes," she said across the room.

"Bring me a stuffed baked potato," McBain said. "Just put everything on it, and I'll pull off whatever I don't like."

"A sound approach," Van Brun said.

The waitress got the potato. Boo followed her out of the kitchen. He pulled up a chair and introduced himself to McBain and Van Brun. "I just now ate two free lunches," he said.

"I suspect those were mine," Van Brun said.

"They're mine now," Boo said.

"Boo," I said. "Have you heard of a Kronmiller farm?"

"Mm. By Kronmiller Mountain."

"You know the place?"

"Sure. Dad and I used to run dogs there."

"Do you remember a boarded-up cabin on the premises?"

"Log cabin?"

"Yes!"

"Sure, on the mountain," Boo said. "Somebody used to live there long ago."

"Take me there immediately," I said. I stood up.

"We'll wait for Ms. McBain to finish her potato," Van Brun said.

McBain bobbed her head and gave a little wave. Her mouth was full. I sat back down. She had chosen this moment to eat a hearty meal. She wielded the fork with her right hand and gripped the potato with her left. She hunched over the plate like a pup over its food bowl, shielding it with her bony shoulders. She snaked out a thin arm and grabbed a glass of something to drink.

Boo leaned back, turning his chair to one side, and crossed his legs. He groaned. "I'm as full as a bug," he said. He bumped the brim of his cap with a knuckle.

He got up and went to the kitchen, and he came back with a tall paper cup. It was empty. He pulled two napkins from the dispenser on the table and wadded them at the bottom of the cup, and then he took some tobacco from the round container he carried in the right rear pocket of his overalls and loaded his bottom lip with it. Van Brun observed with amusement. McBain, when she saw what Boo was doing, stared at him wordlessly. Her fork plinked the edge of her plate.

Boo put his lips to the cup rim and strained his chin in a certain way. A bit of coffee-colored liquid dribbled out.

Now it was McBain's turn to reach for the chrome-plated napkin dispenser. She held a napkin to her face and emptied the partly chewed contents of her mouth into it. She wrapped the starchy bolus closely and set it on the table. The meal was over now. "I'm ready to leave," she said.

I asked her if she intended to come with us to the cabin.

"Please join us," Van Brun cooed.

"I may as well," McBain said. "What else am I going to do?"

"You may find our little discovery newsworthy," Van Brun said.

"I'm doubtful of that," she said. She produced a credit card from her slender purse, and Van Brun pretended alarm. "You must allow me this small privilege," he said.

"It's a business expense," McBain said.

"Ah, but it would mean something to me," Van Brun said.

"It's a two-dollar potato!" Boo said.

"This from a man who has lunched on my leavings," Van Brun said.

Boo shrugged and spit into his cup. McBain let Van Brun pay.

"Although Johnson was a minor president," Van Brun said—the four of us were waiting at the cash register now, and he spoke softly towards McBain as though he did not mean for me to hear—"it is not inconceivable that we shall find things in this cabin that will be of real interest to a great many Americans."

"Like what?" McBain said. She was trying to work the gum machine.

"Well. Items relating to Johnson's impeachment, perhaps, or to his effort to avert the reconstruction of the South. With the war over and the Union preserved, you see, President Johnson was keen to get southern state governments back in the hands of white southerners as promptly as possible. He would never have been impeached, had he not taken the hard line he did against federal civil rights."

McBain mimed a yawn.

"Yes. And then, one of the more sensational possibilities would be—well, I suppose you're familiar, Ms. McBain, with the question of the missing eighteen pages."

"Oh, please," I said. "Don't be ridiculous, Van Brun."

"What eighteen pages?" McBain said.

He winked mysteriously at McBain and said no more, presenting the waitress with a large tip and a formal bow. Then he held the door and waved us out into the parking lot. Only here, as though he must not be overheard, would he continue.

"I refer, my dear, to the eighteen missing pages from the diary of John Wilkes Booth."

McBain was startled. I imagined I could read her mind. She was thinking, *John Wilkes Booth—I've heard that name.*

She recovered her look of disinterest. "I never knew that guy was a diarist," she said.

"He became one in the final days of his life," Van

Brun said. "It's a small date book, actually, bound in red leather, discovered in his pocket soon after he was shot through the neck by Sergeant Corbett."

"Ignore him, McBain," I said. "I know where he's going, and it's nonsense—a cheap conspiracy theory."

Van Brun ignored me. "In the diary Booth describes his escape and his motives," he said. "He styles himself a Brutus, saving the republic from a tyrant. He does clearly allude to a conspiracy and a sudden change of plans, and then a betrayal."

"How is it that pages are missing?" McBain asked him.

"The whole diary was missing for two years," Van Brun said. "It turned up in a file in the War Department in 1867, with pages torn out. The House was considering articles of impeachment, and the obvious questions arose— Who spoliated that book? Who had access to it? Who might have been incriminated? Who stood to benefit most immediately from the murder of President Lincoln?"

"Those charges are as irresponsible now as they were in 1867," I said.

"Right, John," Van Brun said. "And Rose Mary Woods forgot to take her foot off the tape machine pedal."

"Slow down," McBain said. "This is interesting."

"There is absolutely no reason to suppose that Andrew Johnson tore those pages from the diary," I said.

"Booth corresponded with Johnson on the night of the assassination," Van Brun said.

"He left a note at the desk of Johnson's hotel. That proves nothing."

"*Someone* tore the pages out," Van Brun said.

"It might have been Booth," I said.

"But why?" Van Brun said. "Booth *wrote* the pages."

"But here's the main point," I said. "Colonel Conger took the diary from Booth's pocket, and he gave it to Baker at the War Department, and Baker turned it over to Edwin Stanton. Stanton had custody of the thing for two years, and he was Johnson's hated enemy! If there'd been anything even slightly incriminating to Johnson in those pages or in the handling of the diary, you can be very sure that Edwin Stanton would have informed the Congress of that fact."

"Not if it incriminated Stanton as well," Van Brun said.

"That's absurd! Stanton was Lincoln's war secretary! He had nothing to gain from an assassination."

"So you suppose," Van Brun said. "But Stanton and Lincoln hadn't always been friends. Stanton spied on him for Buchanan. In later years, Stanton turned his back on President Grant. Stanton was an opportunist."

McBain was rapt, and so was Boo. Van Brun glowed dully. He knew he was torturing the facts—while the scenario he imagined was not an impossible one, it was very unlikely. He certainly hadn't talked this way in Nashville, when I first let him know about Martha Patterson's letter.

Of course, at that time he'd been trying to throw me off Johnson's trail altogether.

"There's no way Booth's pages could be in the purple scrapbook," I said. "Martha Patterson went to her grave believing her father to have been the greatest American since General George Washington. If she had known—as you suppose—that her father had a role in the conspiracy to assassinate Lincoln, she could not have revered him as she did. She preserved his home and made his tailor shop into a shrine."

"I don't know what she knew," Van Brun said, "nor what her feelings might have been when she heard the news of Lincoln's death. What I do know is that she had lived through a long and bloody civil war, and being the daughter of the president meant very much to her. That house she preserved in Greeneville was used as a whorehouse under Confederate occupation, you know."

"A whorehouse!" McBain said.

"Oh yes," Van Brun said. "During the war, the Johnson home became a notorious Negro brothel. That must have stung the pride of this *racist* white tailor-president and his family. But I will also point out to you, John, that it is very likely no one but Winfield Lewis ever guessed where the eighteen pages in Johnson's purple scrapbook had been torn *from*. One does not sign one's name in the pages of one's diary, and the incriminating passage might appear quite innocuous, taken out of its context—'I met with Johnson and he told me to proceed,' for example. Lewis's guess would have been enough to cause him to warn Mrs. Patterson vaguely that the scrapbook must never become part of the Johnson record, but the only way that he or anyone could have known for certain would have been to compare the torn edges to those in the diary itself, which would have been impossible in

Lewis's day. At present, of course, it would be easy enough, since Booth's diary is on display under glass at the Ford's Theater Museum in Washington."

"This is a fantastical invention," I said.

"But suppose for a moment it's true," Van Brun said. "Will you?"

"No."

"I will," McBain said.

"I will," Boo said.

"Supposing it's true, it really rather all makes sense, doesn't it? In fact, it's surprising that no one put it together before. The only missing link was the location of the scrapbook, which we now know, thanks to my years-long intimate relationship with Mrs. Edna Johnson."

"Let's check that shack, Tolley," McBain said.

I thought quickly. The others stood in a horseshoe pattern around me—huge Van Brun, small Boo, and small but large-behaving McBain. I don't think well when people are staring at me, but I had no choice. I had to act quickly now. Van Brun, this fat, dissembling bag of nasty treats, was preparing to steal the credit for a discovery that ought to be mine. My own hopes, I saw, meant nothing to anyone but me. McBain didn't care—she wanted a good story, period. I could see it all playing out, in the very near future: Van Brun on cable television, his face heavily powdered, dropping the biggest bombshell ever dropped by an American historian: The President Killed the President.

I couldn't let it happen. I spoke.

23

"ALL RIGHT," I SAID. "Let's check out the cabin." I looked down at my wing tips. "But first I want to go by the house and change into my boots. This may involve some hiking."

"You're right about that," Boo said. "Everybody needs to be dressed for the land."

McBain went into the back seat of her rental car and exchanged her heels for the running shoes.

"What about you?" Boo said, looking at Van Brun's feet. I studiously did not look at them. I was already on the edge of being sick.

"I go everywhere in my sandals," Van Brun said. "I'm like a Roman that way."

It was agreed we would caravan to Boo's, and from there to the cabin. I rode with Boo in his truck. I asked him whether he owned a video camera.

"Nope."

"What about just a regular camera?" I said.

"Well of course. Everybody's got one of them."

"Do you know where it is?"

"In a wicker basket by my chair under a newspaper that I'm saving."

"What about some binoculars?"

"On the strap by the door."

"Have you fed your dogs?"

"Yes."

"Do you have a first-aid kit?"

"Not per se. I have the makings of one," he said.

"We'll definitely be needing a complete first-aid kit for the hike to the cabin," I said. "There will no doubt be rusty metal, splinters, old farm tools, and probably wild rats and mice."

"I'd say there will be all that and more. Don't forget the snakes, John."

"Do you have a snakebite kit?"

"Oh yes."

"We'll be needing that as well. How long do you think it will take you to assemble these items?"

"Give me ten minutes."

"Okay," I said.

At the house, Boo ran inside. Van Brun and McBain parked across the road, by the barn. Van Brun stepped out of his car and said, "Is this where Mr. Boo lives?"

"Tolley lives here too," McBain said. "In a run-down house on the hill."

"This is characteristic East Tennessee," Van Brun said.

"The country is formed primarily of eighty-million-

year-old limestone deposits," I said. I'd invented the figure on the spot. "The bedrock is channeled with craggy
chasms and underground passageways. Come quickly
and let me show you what I'm referring to. Boo will be a
few minutes inside."

Unsuspectingly they followed me into the woods.
McBain asked if there were ticks.

"Not at this time of year," I said.

"It's June," she said.

"A Tennessee tick is a harmless passenger," Van Brun
said.

I led them to the mouth of Boo's listening station,
where the top of the ladder protruded. I climbed down.
"This opening in the ground was used by Indians and
early settlers for the storage of apples and root crops," I
called up to them. "The floor is scattered with bits of
ancient crockery. The air remains a constant sixty-eight
degrees. Come on down quickly and have a look while we
wait."

Looking up I saw McBain's head and her fair hair
with a halo of light at its outline. "What are you doing
down there, Tolley?"

"Looking for potsherds," I said. "There's also a stream
with blind fish in it."

"What the hell," McBain said. She was down in seven
steps, and she turned to me and grinned. "Wow, a cave,"
she said. "Why is there a futon?"

"Come down, Van Brun," I said.

"I question whether that ladder will safely carry a
man my size," he said.

"It's a good ladder made of heavy aluminum," I said.

McBain had picked up a *Nose Dog* from the futon and held it up towards the light that came from the opening. "This is weird," she said.

Van Brun started down the ladder. It creaked, but he had rather risk death or injury than be left out of the party. I had calculated as much. He was soon below ground with us, panting wetly, using up air. "My gracious," he said. "It's homey down here, but dark."

"I should have brought the flashlight," I said. "I'll run get it."

"Danielle?" Van Brun said. "What are you reading, my dear?"

I went quickly up the ladder.

"Tolley? Where are you going?" McBain said. "Big guy, grab his leg!"

"Big guy?" Van Brun said.

She had guessed my plan—but it was too late. I pulled the ladder up behind me and threw it aside. I looked down into the hole. Van Brun squinted up at me, shielding his eyes. McBain appeared beside him. "Tolley, you weaselly son of a bitch," she said. "You won't go through with this. It's not your style."

"If it's not my style, why did you tell Van Brun to grab my leg?"

She considered. "Damn it!" she said.

There was a chirping noise from the hole, like the sound of crickets. Van Brun jumped and patted his clothes all over. McBain produced a cell phone from somewhere on her person. "Hello?" she said. "Jerry!"

Van Brun stopped patting. "Now I wish I'd eaten lunch," he said.

McBain waved her free hand, shushing him. "No, I've got a minute," she said into the phone.

I got back to the truck just as Boo was exiting the house. The camera hung from his shoulder and the binoculars from his neck. He had a shoe box under his arm. "I got bandages, alcohol, iodine, needle and thread, sterile gauze, and adhesive tape," he said. "I couldn't find my snakebite kit. I may have used it."

"Excellent. Very good," I said.

"Can you think of anything else we need?"

"Not a thing. We're well provided for."

"Where is Tweedledee and Tweedledon't?"

"They went up to the knob," I said.

"I thought we was in a hurry."

"They're going to stay," I said. "They want to be alone."

"Oh, yuck. You can't be serious."

"I am, Boo." We got into the truck and left.

"She's cute, but that big old boy's too much for me," Boo said. "I wouldn't have never put them two together."

"I'm just going to shut my eyes, if you don't mind," I said. If the preseizure aura state began, I would not be able to stop it. I told myself that I was in a pleasant, comfortable place. *A study carrel.*

"Oh no," Boo said. He brought the truck to a screeching stop in the road. "You're not going to believe what I'm about to point out to you!" he said.

"What?"

"You forgot to change into your boots."

I closed my eyes again and buckled my seat belt. "Let's go on anyway," I said.

We drove on. I noticed my own breathing and paid attention to keeping it steady and smooth. Once one pays attention to one's breathing, it is hard to stop thinking about it. I waited for the automatic breathing to resume, but it didn't, and I had to keep breathing on purpose.

"I'm going to be famous," I said to Boo.

"Remember me then," he said.

We were soon away from the neighborhood that I had become familiar with. We drove a winding road along a creek that was shaded by tall sycamores, and then the creek went underground. I asked Boo how far off the place was.

"Another ten miles or more," he said. "Then we walk a ways. That's assuming they haven't paved it all in the last twenty years."

"You haven't been here in that long?"

"Nope."

I sat thinking nothing until it occurred to me that we had been riding already for more than twenty minutes. "Boo, this is outside your radius."

He faced straight ahead and did not look at me. "I know it, John."

A few long seconds went by, and then he let out a voluble whoop.

"Easy there," I said.

He let a second whoop go. This one was longer, with a fillip at the end.

I suggested he let me drive.

"No, I'm perfectly in control," he said. "Fear is just a feeling, John."

He was right, of course. We see this fact illustrated not only in the phobic neuroses that torment so many otherwise reasonable people—fear of spiders, fear of elevators, fear of thread, fear of brushing against another person's body, fear of falling from a window—but also in the equally irrational bursts of fearlessness that have been observed from time to time among soldiers who are facing the genuine prospect of death. An example is the run up Missionary Ridge made by Thomas's troops on the morning of November 25, 1863—an episode often recounted in the pages of *Civil War Days*. No responsible commander could have ordered this reckless assault: it was spontaneous. Indifferent to death, Thomas's men succeeded in dislodging the Confederate forces from Lookout Mountain. One may cite examples from everyday life as well in which persons have met with unlikely success through unwarranted bravery.

One's fears are seldom proportional to the threat, it seems. Often a person is too afraid, and just as often, not nearly afraid enough. He considers the abyss of history with the same brain he used to consider his angry girlfriend or unhappy landlady. Sometimes the soul feels a chill when it ought to be frozen solid.

Boo pulled off the pavement and onto a track between fence posts. It looked like nothing more than a wide trail. The grade was steep, and Boo eased the truck up it until we came to a dead tree that had fallen across the way. We got out and stepped around to the front of the truck. A white cotton brassiere had been laid across the tree. Leaves had fallen on the brassiere, been rained on, and dried.

Boo straddled the tree, then lifted his other leg and crossed. I followed.

"This road has fallen out of use," Boo said.

"At any rate it is not used for traveling."

We had climbed a good ways up the steep track before I noticed that I was still wearing my tweed jacket. I didn't want to go back to the truck now. The woods were cool, with a high, thick canopy of poplar, oak, and locust. My smooth-soled shoes slid on the damp, leafy ground. My mouth was dry. "We should have brought water," I said to Boo.

"Think about something else," he said from ahead of me.

The trail disappeared. We headed upwards. There was not much brush—a few clumps of rhododendron here and there, and scattered violets underfoot, some purple and some white. I had to stop to catch my breath more than once. I thought uneasily of McBain and Van Brun. She had her cell phone and would long since have called 911. I couldn't go back to Boo's. Was it kidnapping to trap people in a cave? But there was no reason to go back. I had Zimmer's Visa, which would get me some cash from an ATM, and I'd use the cash for a bus ticket, to Canada maybe. I'd ride to Toronto with the purple scrapbook on my lap.

I was slow. Boo would have made better time uphill without me. We passed through a stand of dead hemlocks with the bark dropping off. I thought of the men who had left their farms and come to the mountains to wait out the war and avoid being pressed into service by one side or the other. Brave men, perhaps, who wanted to be left alone.

"There it is," Boo said.

I'd been looking almost directly at it, and yet I hadn't seen it there. It was a dark shape not more than twelve feet wide, a single story high. It was built up off the ground on rocks. There was a window, with the glass broken; the front door was shut. The roof was metal and heavily oxidized, but it appeared to be intact.

Boo stood with his arms folded, looking up into the trees purposefully.

"Let's go in," I said.

"You go first."

I ran up. The front steps were missing, and the doorsill was at my knees. I turned the knob and the door stuck, then came open.

I saw a dusty board floor with rags on it. There was a powerful smell of musk and ammonia. I tested the floor for solidness, then pulled myself up.

A bird flew out of a stovepipe end and circled the room. I ducked, and it went out the door past my head.

There was just the one room, with one window. The walls had been papered over with printed text. My heart stopped for a moment. Was this what had come of Johnson's purple scrapbook? But it was only the Greeneville newspaper, from circa 1900.

There was no cupboard, no closet—no promise-filled

steamer trunk to knock the lock off of. There was a wooden crate in one corner with some brown bottles and a mammal's nest in it. There was a gnawed ladder-back chair against the wall, and there was a cot under the window with a green cotton bedspread wadded on top.

I moved the bedspread, which was rigid. There was nothing under it.

The cot had a thin mattress on it, covered in blue-and-white ticking and stained. There were springs under the mattress, and I tried to peer under the cot but couldn't see much. The floor was filthy with animal droppings and dust. I grabbed the mattress by the edge with both hands, and holding my breath, I flipped it off of the cot and onto the floor. It landed flat, and the room filled with a dusty cloud.

Against the cot springs was a small pile of books. They were magazines, actually—three of them, each about six by eight inches in size, with black-and-white cover art and green display type. I picked up the one on top. It was a magazine called the *American Naturist*, volume 12, number 3, August 1947. The cover illustration showed a middle-aged female naturist pushing a vacuum cleaner in her living room.

"John?"

I turned. Boo was at the doorway, standing on the ground.

"Did you find your Johnson pages?" he said.

"I found this," I said. "It's—"

"That don't look much like historical materials," Boo said. "I see headlights."

I dropped the magazine back onto the pile.

"Hey, John, listen up."

"What?"

"Are you my friend?"

"Yes," I said.

"Do you want to help me out?"

"Sure, Boo." I was a little confused by the moment. Dazed.

Boo took the cell phone from the thigh pocket of his overalls and held it out to me. "I'm leaving," he said. "In forty-five minutes, no sooner, I want you to call the fire station. Tell them there's a fire and tell them to page me."

I took the phone.

"What's the number?" I said.

"It's under Contacts," he said. "Do you know how to find that? Here, let me show you." He took the phone back and showed me how to punch through to CONTACTS and to the heading PVFD. "Got it?"

"Yes." I took the phone back. "Why are we doing this?"

"Just tell them Kronmiller Mountain," he said. "Make sure they page me."

"There's some smoke behind you," I said. I pointed, and Boo turned and looked. It was coming from the ground, fifty yards off. I saw a smudge of orange.

"I know it," Boo said. "That's why you're calling. So we can come put the fire out."

"Why don't you put the fire out right now?"

"I just now made the fire," Boo said.

I looked at him. "I don't understand."

"Look, John. I don't want to talk a great deal about this, so I'd like you to just understand me. If I go over to that fire right now, I could step on it with my shoe, and it would go out. But that's not a *fire call*, is it? It's not a fire call until somebody calls it in."

"Why don't we call it in right now?"

"Because I want them to *page me*, John," he said, patting his chest pocket. "Also it's still too little."

I watched the rising smoke. There wasn't much breeze, and the smoke rose straight.

"I understand," I said.

"Good. Can I count on you, buddy?"

"Yes."

"Thanks. You're my bud." He gave a hoot and ran off down the mountain, stopping only to check the fire briefly and lay a branch across it before he was gone.

24

THINGS WEREN'T LOOKING so good now. I had dust in my nose, and I have a pretty vivid imagination when it comes to sources of dust. Most dust is dander, and I'll say no more. I jumped down out of the filthy, depressing cabin and put some quick distance between it and myself, then got out my handkerchief and blew my nose like there would be no tomorrow. I wiped my face and hands with some leaves from the ground.

I couldn't think what sort of person would ever have chosen to live up here. Snakes are built for solitude, but a human needs to get himself seen by other humans from time to time for the good of his mental health, even if he doesn't enjoy it.

I walked through the woods behind the cabin a little ways and came to a very large gray boulder with whitish blooms of lichen the size of saucers on it. The boulder was twice my height. I thought about bashing my brains out against the rock, but it was only a sterile idea—I knew I didn't have the sort of disposition that goes in for suicide. My nature was gloomy, but I clung to life like a burr. I was a great lover of the minor domestic comforts—a shelf of books, a big bowl of cold cereal. This business of luring McBain and Van Brun down a hole was destined, I had a feeling, to be the one really large spontaneous gesture of my life. I was a little relieved to think so.

My mood became meditative as I reflected on the ups and downs that characterize the progress of every person's career on this planet. Around me I heard the calls of various songbirds, each male seeking a mate of his own species. Laying my hand on the surface of the boulder, I felt a coolness emanating from very deep. It would take all summer long to warm a stone of this size, and then all winter to cool it down again. Even the stone had its moods, though they came and went slowly.

I hadn't thought of the time and was startled when Boo's cell phone rang. I got it out of my coat pocket and after several rings figured out how to answer it.

"Was you going to call or not?" Boo said.

"I was. Hang up and I'll call you now."

"Never mind. I want to change plans."

"Okay," I said. "What are we doing?"

"There's a problem on my end," Boo said. "I can't come back out there, John."

"Sure you can," I said.

"No I can't. My heart's about to jump out of my shirt."

I told him to take a breath. "Where are you?"

"I'm under my bed."

"Why?"

"I'm settling down. Brownie's here. But look. The trip back was not good, John."

"Did you panic?"

"Oh buddy. Nausea, trembling, the whole kit and caboodle."

He was quiet.

"We all have our limits," I said.

"Amen, brother. How's that fire?"

I had forgotten it. I stepped over to the other side of the cabin for a look.

"Boo! The fire is large!"

"How large?"

"I don't know! As big as a house!"

"Whose house?"

I ran closer. The flames were twice my height, and the smoke was thick. A breeze moved. "I'm going to hang up and call nine-one-one," I said.

"Hold on there, John. I'd rather you not."

"Why?"

"Well, how are you going to tell them it started?"

"I don't know. I'll say I just found it."

"You'll need to do better than that, John."

"I'll tell them my campfire got out of control."

"You go camping in a sport coat and street shoes?"

"I'll strip naked," I said.

"John, if the law finds out I lit that fire, my butt will be back in Brushy Mountain, in the pen. I don't want to go there, okay?"

The fire was cracking and sucking air loudly. I asked Boo what he wanted me to do.

"Put it out," he said.

"How?"

"Deprive it of its fuel."

I pulled what fallen wood lay nearby and hadn't caught yet away from the fire. Then I got as close as I could and started kicking leaves and sticks around. The litter of leaves was wet underneath, but dry on top. I used my feet to clear a track around the edge of the fire, scratching at the ground like a chicken. "It's spreading," I said to Boo. A sort of fire peninsula had formed, and there was a large patch of low flames at the other end of it. "This is insane," I said.

"How's the wind?"

"There's some wind. It's blowing."

"Watch the wind," he said.

I told him I would call him back.

"Let me call you back, because it's cheaper," he said. He hung up.

I emptied the pockets of my Osim Lowe jacket and used it to grab a burning branch and drag it into an open area. The tallest part of the fire was too hot to go near: there was a dead tree that would have to burn itself out. I used the jacket to beat down the lower flames as they threatened to spread.

In a few minutes Boo's phone rang. "Is it out?"

"It's better," I said. "Is somebody coming to get me?"

"I'm sending Dweena."

"Dweena?"

"My cousin," Boo said. "Are you ready for her?"

"Can't you send somebody else?"

"Who, John?"

There wasn't anyone else to send. Not Dwayne. "Okay," I said.

"Should I send her now, or do you need some more time with the fire?"

"A little more time," I said. "It's burning out."

"Okay. Safety first."

"Boo, I've got something to tell you," I said.

"What?"

"McBain and Van Brun went down in your listening station. They may still be down there."

"Why?"

"I didn't want them following us, so I lured them in."

"But they weren't going to follow us. You said they were up at your house being friendly."

"I lied. They didn't follow us because I pulled the ladder up."

There was a silence, then Boo said, "I see I'm still getting to know you, John."

25

I FOUND A WASHTUB under the cabin, and I used it to scrape out a shallow trench around the fire. Then I went around again and made the trench wider. The fire was controlled. I threw the ruined jacket in and let it burn. Then I went down the mountain and waited for Dweena. I tossed the brassiere in the bushes and sat on the log.

When Dweena arrived in her white Wagoneer, she was wearing wire-rimmed glasses. Her dark brown hair was uncollected or loose. It hung straight, that is to say. It shone. She blinked at me.

"I didn't know you wore glasses," I said.

"What else don't you know?"

"I don't know."

"Did you find your Johnson papers?"

"No. Didn't Boo tell you?"

"I had trouble making sense out of what Boo said, and I think I don't want it explained. He told me you were looking for the Kronmiller farm."

I got in on the passenger side. It was late, and the mail-delivering day was over. She drove from behind the wheel. "We found it," I said. "It was a bust."

She nodded, and we headed out. "So what are you doing here?" she said.

"This is Kronmiller Mountain, right?"

"Yes. But the farm was not on the mountain."

"Where was it?"

"In the hollow," she said.

"Can you take me there?"

She pulled over and turned the Wagoneer around.

Beyond the track where Boo had pulled off we rounded a turn and came to a new subdivision with two- and three-story houses set high on top of multiple-bay garages. The lots were small and treeless, with short concrete driveways.

"It won't be that easy to get to," she said.

Why should it be? was my thought.

We passed an electrical switching station, fenced in by chain link. Dweena turned onto a side road past a sign that said "Tennessee Valley Authority." We rode through some woods, then past a parking lot, then past another sign that said "Boat Ramp." We came to the end of the road, where she parked. We got out of the Wagoneer and crossed some freshly mowed grass to the edge of a bluff. Dweena pointed into the water.

"That's the hollow," she said.

The hollow was now a lake. Low sunlight flashed on its surface. There were wooded hills all around, except to the right, where the dam was.

"When did they flood it?" I said.

"In the fifties. Dwayne could tell you more."

"Mm."

"In school we used to take field trips to the dam," she said. "You can walk inside the generators."

"That must have been exciting."

"Well, they didn't let us do it. The TVA man went inside."

"Are the buildings still there, under the water? The farm buildings and so on?"

"They didn't move them, if that's what you mean. But if it was made out of wood, it floated."

"Of course it did. I guess this concludes my search for Andrew Johnson's purple scrapbook," I said.

We stood awhile. I asked her if she knew why Johnson ran off from his apprenticeship in North Carolina.

"No."

"A woman was going to prosecute him for throwing clods of dirt at her house."

"Hm."

"He had a crush on this woman's daughter," I explained.

"Oh. I get it."

"Sometimes it's hard for a young person to say what he feels."

She looked at me. "I wish you the best in all your undertakings, John."

I thanked her.

"You're welcome."

"Stay away from Mike Signet," I said.

"What?"

"Stay away from Mike Signet and Ronnie, and disinvolve yourself from any business your uncle Dwayne may have undertaken with Signet. Something's going on that you don't know about, but you're probably going to hear about it soon." I recalled that the last time I saw McBain, she was on the phone with a producer from *Point Blank*.

"What in the world are you talking about?" Dweena said.

"That's all I'm going to say." Through the lenses I studied her eyes. "I'm trying to be your friend," I said. I went back to the Wagoneer and got in it.

She got in behind the wheel, and we left. "Don't you think I know these people better than you do?"

"I don't pretend to know them," I said. "I just know things about them."

"Dwayne says you're leaving Tennessee."

"I am," I said. "What else did he tell you?"

"He told me you're unhappy with him."

"That's true, too. But I don't want to talk about it with you."

"Why not?"

"Because I don't want to damage some illusions you may have about your uncle."

"I don't have illusions about Dwayne," she said. "He has vices I don't approve of. Where are you going?"

"I don't know. New York, California—it doesn't really matter."

I watched trees go by out the window. At the switching station I spotted an owl on top of a transformer. Unusual in broad daylight, I thought. But it was a plastic owl, put there to keep squirrels and birds from nesting.

"You're strange, aren't you?" Dweena said.

"Yes I am," I said. "You're a bit odd, too."

"Am I?"

"Sure. You're into your twenties, yet live with your cousin. You're extremely shy, to the point of being difficult to talk to sometimes."

She nodded slowly, looking ahead.

"I don't see why you don't get out and maybe put a dress on, I don't know. You're always in boots and coveralls. You look pretty in your glasses, which is strange in itself, the reverse of what one expects. Do you normally wear contact lenses?"

"Yes," she said, a little huskily.

"Okay. Like Boo. Well. I don't mean to be blunt."

"It's fine," she said. "I'm just shy, I'm not sensitive."

"What's your puzzle of?"

"I beg your pardon?"

"I saw that you're working a jigsaw puzzle," I said. "I couldn't see what it was of, because of the glare, and since I wasn't invited in."

"It's a building in Switzerland," she said. "A chalet, or something. Who cares?" She looked at me, red-eyed. "What is it you think you know about Dwayne and Mike?"

"I'm not going to tell you," I said. "It's not only chicken fighting."

"Tell me," she said.

"No. I shouldn't have mentioned it, maybe."

She swerved the Wagoneer to the side of the road and came to a hard stop. "Tell me or get out," she said.

That wasn't much of a choice. I told her.

"I don't believe that," she said. She pulled back onto the road.

"I can't help what you believe," I said. "I saw them together, and I watched Boo burn the mail. I confronted your uncle and he admitted it."

She flashed another look at me. "Dwayne admitted it?"

"Yes."

I had said too much, I saw. I was repentant now, but it was too late. Dweena got the last word. "I wish you'd just married that girl and stayed in Ohio," she said.

26

S HE DROPPED ME OFF at Boo's driveway, then
backed out and left.

McBain's and Van Brun's cars were gone, and Boo
didn't answer when I knocked at the carport door. I
walked up to the knob, where I was disappointed to find
Van Brun's brown Volvo parked on the grass. Van Brun
himself reclined on my daybed, reading the back of a
cereal box as he ate from it with his hand. He inserted
the hand up to the wrist and I heard him rattling the
cereal with his fingers before he pulled the hand out and
brought it to his mouth. So much for that box of cereal, I
thought. He could have the whole thing now because I
wouldn't be eating any more of it.

"Yes, I have made myself at home, he said. "I think
we're beyond formalities now, Tolley."

I went to the kitchen and got a jug of water from the
refrigerator. I drank what was in it, about a fifth of a gal-
lon. I went back to the front room.

"Get out," I said. "I never want to see you again."

"I wish I had some sweet milk," Van Brun said.

"I'm all out."

"Perhaps Mr. Boo has some."

"I apologize for leaving you underground," I said.

"I acknowledge your apology, though I reserve the right to take legal recourse at any time in the future. I haven't yet called my attorney, because I can't find your telephone."

"I don't have a telephone," I said. I asked him how he got out of the cave.

"I lifted Ms. McBain out, and she lowered the ladder to me. She's as light as a pen, by the way."

"Where is she?"

"The network has called her back to Manhattan. Some poor fellow's under indictment there—Innsberg? Ellsberg? A naturalized Swede."

"Tor Wennerberg?"

"Could be. A big break for Ms. McBain, evidently. Good lord, that young woman is radiant when she's angry."

"I would call her if I had her number," I said.

"You don't have a telephone."

I brought Boo's cell phone from my trouser pocket.

Van Brun put two fingers in his shirt pocket and brought out a business card.

"Thanks," I said, reaching.

"Ah!" He retracted the card. "You may read from the card without touching," he said.

I read it and punched in the number. Van Brun returned the card to his pocket and patted it.

Her phone rang once. "McBain!" she said.

"I apologize for leaving you in a cave," I said.

"Who is this? Tolley?"

"Yes. I heard about Tor Wennerberg's indictment."

"Whose?"

"Tor Wennerberg. The Swede."

"I don't know what you're talking about," she said. "Guess what! Jerry Hedberg's in jail."

"He is?"

"Well, no. His wife bailed him out. He was arrested for setting her car on fire."

"Why?"

"Because it's illegal."

I was confused. "Jerry Hedberg called you to cover his own arrest?"

"No. *Point Blank* won't be covering that story, John. Jerry called me to cover his desk while he goes into detox. I'm temping again."

"Van Brun told me this concerned a naturalized Swede."

"Yes, Jerry used to be Swedish. Have you got something against the Swedish-Americans?"

"No," I said. "I get it now."

"I'd love to answer more questions, but we're about to fly and I've got to switch my phone off."

"Good-bye," I said.

With a click the call ended.

"Rice Krispy?" Van Brun said. He offered the box.

"No thank you," I said. I went to the kitchen and got a bag of peanuts from behind some books. I brought them back to the front room and sat down on the floor.

"Where did you find those?" Van Brun said.

"In my kitchen."

He extended a shiny, fat paw and I gave him some peanuts.

"I take it you didn't find your purple Johnson scrapbook," Van Brun said.

"You don't sound surprised."

"And I'm not. You just never struck me as the lucky type, Tolley."

Boo walked in, followed by Brownie. "John, I hate to bring this up, but tomorrow's the first of the month," he said.

"So?"

"Rent's due."

"Oh. Boo, it's been nice living here, but I've decided——"

His phone rang in my pocket. I took it out, and Boo took it from my hand. "Hello? I don't know. Let me see if I can find him." He lowered the phone, carefully pressing his thumb over the little row of holes into which one spoke. "May I see you on the porch, John?"

I followed him out.

"This is Dwayne," Boo said. "Are you ready to speak to him?"

"Yes."

"First tell me what you were doing this afternoon," Boo said.

"You know what I was doing."

"Tell me."

"I was on a mountain putting out the fire you started."

"Wrong. Try again."

"I'm not good at lying, Boo."

"Don't lie. *Withhold.*"

"Okay."

"So what did you do this afternoon, John?"

"I ran into an old acquaintance, and then we ate some peanuts."

He gave me the phone.

"Hello," I said.

"My niece is upset, young John. *Very* upset."

"I know, and I'm sorry."

"You don't know, and you can never be sorry enough to suit me. I'm going to explain something to you, and I want you to listen closely, because you're going to be satisfied, and in return you are going to promise me you will never, not damned ever, repeat what I am going to tell you. Not to anyone, including me, and including yourself. Do you follow?"

"I don't know," I said.

"The mail you saw Boo burning was mine."

"Huh?"

"My mail, John. I made it, made the copies, sorted and labeled it, and so forth. All me. My expense. Upright Tennesseans Thinking of the Children is myself."

"You're trying to stop the lottery?"

"No, John. I don't care about the lottery. Do you?"

"Well, I—"

"Never mind. I don't care whether you care."

"I don't get it," I said.

"I know. That's why I'm explaining it for you. Mike Signet paid me not to deliver my own mail."

"Why in the world would he do that?"

"Because he didn't know it was mine."

"You mean you printed the flyers for the purpose of having him bribe you not to mail them?"

"Exactly. That's the size of it."

"Why?"

"Two reasons. One, for the money, and two, because I just don't like the man."

"If you're making this up, it's some lie," I said.

"It's no lie. Now, remember your promise, and in the future, when in doubt, clam. And don't upset my niece anymore." He hung up.

Boo had gone inside, and I did too. Boo took his phone from me and slid it into the thigh pocket of his overalls.

Brownie was on the daybed with Van Brun. Van Brun asked if I had some fingernail scissors he could borrow.

"No."

"Would you like some Rice Krispies, pretty?" Van Brun said to the dog.

"Brownie, no," Boo said.

Brownie looked at Boo, then at Van Brun's cupped hand, which had cereal in it. She didn't move.

I asked Boo to let me borrow his phone again.

He took it from his pocket and looked at it. "Battery's low," he said. "So are my minutes."

"It's the end of the month," Van Brun reminded him. "You need to use your minutes."

Boo gave me the phone. I punched through to CON-TACTS.

"Who are you calling?" Boo said.

He and Van Brun stared at me.

I went back out to the porch and punched through to DWEENA.

27

"I SPOKE TO DWAYNE," Dweena said.

"So did I."

"He wouldn't tell me everything, but it sounds like Mike's going to jail."

"He didn't tell me *that*," I said.

She didn't elaborate. I changed the subject.

"For some time I've been planning a dinner," I said. "Would you be willing to come?"

"Now?"

"No, tomorrow."

"Okay," she said.

The meal was to take place at Boo's house. I was uncertain what to cook and made the mistake of mentioning this in front of Van Brun, who offered to prepare the meal. I refused but Boo insisted that we let him. "Let's see what the man can do," he said.

Twenty-five hours later, Dweena knocked at Boo's carport door. "Who could that be?" Boo said out loud. He went to get it, and from the kitchen I heard him ask loudly, "Why did you knock?"

I couldn't make out the answer.

"Well you never knocked before," Boo said.

Laboriously, Van Brun worked himself up out of his chair. The day had not gone exactly as planned. Van Brun slept late on Boo's sofa while I shopped with his grocery list, and he'd just begun chopping vegetables when he cut his finger and had to be taken to Urgent Care to get it stitched up. It was his left index finger. Since then he had sat in his chair in the kitchen with the finger in its gauze wrapping pointing upwards, giving me instructions. I had chopped his bell peppers, slivered his garlic, crushed his mint leaves, and roasted his mustard in oil. I never saw the point of making a lengthy ritual out of food preparation, with the exception of hickory barbecue. On the other hand, I was glad to be the one handling the food, because I knew that my hands had been carefully washed. Not so with Van Brun's. That very morning I'd watched him let a dog lick his face from chin to hairline then sit down to breakfast without so much as rinsing off.

"I am Luke Van Brun at your service," he said to Dweena.

"Hello," she said, scowling.

She had on a blue dress with thin straps, rather tight. She reminded me some of myself in a new suit, with the difference that she was ennobled by the effort instead of looking childish, as I always do in new clothes. Of course I was ashamed to think she had worn the dress because of my comment about her coveralls. However, she looked nice. She was wearing blue heels that matched the dress.

"You got out that curling iron, didn't you?" Boo said.

I busied myself in a cupboard.

"Luke, this is Ronnie," Boo said. "He's one of our law-makers."

Runnels was there, off his crutches and in his postal uniform. I hadn't noticed him at first. He stood in the doorway, silent.

"Very glad, very glad," Van Brun said. "A special honor."

Runnels looked him up and down warily, then dragged his foot into the living room. I heard the television come on.

"Who's cooking?" Dweena said.

"John is performing *sous* duties tonight," Van Brun said liquidly. He waved his hurt finger. "I am the chef in charge." He went to Boo's cupboard, twitching and winking, and brought down four jelly glasses, and then he made a show of lifting a bottle of wine and reading aloud from the label in a sardonic tone. He uncorked the bottle efficiently, in spite of his hurt pointer, and he poured a tiny amount in a glass that he handed to Dweena.

She frowned at it, drank, then nodded and held out her glass for more.

I took a glass too. Boo declined to drink. Van Brun asked him why.

"I haven't cared for alcohol of any sort since I served time in prison," he said.

Van Brun said he failed to perceive the connection.

"There was some boys that made a kind of hooch out of Jolly Ranchers there," he said. "It put me off the stuff."

"I never served time in prison," Van Brun said, "but I did pull two years in the service. They whipped the bashfulness out of me."

We ate the food, which was good. We ate at the kitchen table, then moved into the living room. The local news was on with a picture of Mike Signet, whom the anchorman said had been accused by postmasters in Fall Branch and Erwin of offering them bribes to stop the delivery of antilottery mailers. "Signet, who did not immediately respond to calls from Channel Nine News, is reportedly vacationing in Toronto, Canada."

"That's odd," I said.

"Not in the least," Van Brun said. "Toronto is lovely in summer."

"Old Mikey finally made a misstep," Boo said.

Dweena got up and went into the kitchen.

"I guess this ruins the chances for a lottery in Tennessee," I said.

"That skunk better not have ruined it," Boo said. "I'd like to just be well-off once and for all."

"Tennessee will have its lottery," Van Brun said. "It will be approved in the referendum. That is my prediction."

"I wouldn't be so sure," I said. "When the people find out that their trust has been abused, they respond accordingly."

"That would be the rational thing, but the people aren't rational," Van Brun said. "The people are children who want to play and be entertained."

"Your condescension is stunning."

"I don't condescend in the least," Van Brun said. "The politicians are children, too. We're all irresponsible children. Adulthood is a myth, or rather, a game. I should know—I played professor for thirty years. But I have the keen eye of a child, and I've paid attention. Self-government does exist, but *rational* self-government—whether we're speaking of the polity or of the individual by himself—that does not exist yet, nor do I expect it to. We're too easily distracted, too flighty, too easily bored. The lottery means stimulation, and we will have it, mark my words."

I glanced at Runnels. He was asleep.

"Old Mike set many times where you're now setting," Boo said to me, "eating my chips and drinking my soft drinks."

"Signet did?"

"Yes."

"How'd you get to be friends?"

"He was never my friend. He was my cousin-in-law."

"How was he your cousin-in-law?"

"He married my blood cousin."

I pointed towards the kitchen.

"Everyone makes mistakes," Boo said.

I got up and froze. Then I unfroze and went to the kitchen, where Dweena was standing with her back to the sink, her arms folded over her chest.

"You were married to Mike Signet?"

"I told you that."

"No, you didn't," I said. "You told me you were married, but you never told me to him."

"Do you want me to tell you my whole history, starting before I was born?"

"Yes," I said.

She nodded. "We were in high school, and Mike was ambitious."

"That's enough," I said.

We looked at each other in silence. She lowered her eyebrows, and slowly, she turned her back to me.

What was this? I took five steps closer to her.

The kitchen door swung open. I jumped. Brownie came in and dropped a bone into her big ceramic bowl. The bowl rang. Brownie looked at me and left.

I drew close again to Dweena Price and smelled her hair. I will say no more about what happened next. I draw the curtain.

The door swung open again. It was Boo this time and he clapped his hands to his eyes. "It's time for the show," he said.

We went back to the living room and took our seats. I will skip over the procedural details of *This Changes Everything,* which are typical for the sort of show it is. The announcer belted out an introduction: "From Pacific Grove, California, Louise Zimmer!" A spotlight rose to illumine her, standing behind a glittered lectern. I happened to know that she was standing on a step stool, but had promised to tell no one.

Boo said, "Oh my gosh. Is that your mother?"

"Yes."

"She looks just like you!"

"She's my mother," I said.

"I know, but I was never prepared for this extent of a resemblance," Boo said. "It's like she's *you*, with makeup and different hair."

"We all come from somewhere," Van Brun said. "John's mother is an attractive woman."

I asked him to say nothing else on those lines.

The contestants were quizzed as a panel, and Mother prevailed in this segment. A lifetime of travel and her diverse domestic history were no hindrance to her, in this game. Quite the reverse. In the next stage she faced a series of questions read quickly by the tanned and cowlicked host.

"If you are William the Bastard, whom are you the duke of?"

"The Normans!" Van Brun cried out.

"If you're wearing a John the Conqueroo, what are you wearing?"

"A root!"

"How do you wear a root?" Boo said.

"In a small sack around your neck or on your belt loop," Van Brun said.

"I am a creature that walks on my stomach. What am I?"

Van Brun: "A gastropod!"

"These gears form a solar system in the transmission of your automobile. What—"

Van Brun cut him off: "Planetary gears!"

"In referring to this commonly used building material, for what do the initials MDF stand?"

"Medium-density fiberboard!"

"We are the shortest and tallest men to serve as United States President, respectively. Name us."

"James Madison and Abraham Lincoln!"

"Joe Turner suspected he had an intestinal parasite, so he visited his iridologist. Where did she look?"

"Into his eyes!"

Mother got this last one wrong, though her answer brought applause from the studio audience.

Van Brun, on the other hand, had answered every question correctly. Boo asked him why he did not move to California and make his living competing on game shows.

"If you'll notice, they don't prefer corpulent retired Ph.D.s on these quiz programs," Van Brun said. It was an admirable bit of self-scrutiny, for which he deserved some credit.

We watched another round of contestants, and then Boo said, "I'm going to let my dogs run."

Brownie got up and went to the door.

"I would like to see this," Van Brun said.

"You don't see it," Boo said. "You hear it."

"I know that," Van Brun said.

"If you know it, why did you say 'I want to see this'?"

"It's a figure of speech."

"Well if you want to do this with me, you're going to have to stop speeching," Boo said.

Van Brun followed Boo outside silently, holding his

bandaged finger aloft. I shook Runnels awake, and he got up and limped off after them.

Dweena grabbed the remote and switched off the television. We looked at each other awhile.

"Welcome to Tennessee," she said.

About the Author

James Whorton, Jr., is the author of *Approximately Heaven*. He was raised in Florida and Mississippi and educated at the University of Southern Mississippi, Johns Hopkins, and the University of Wales. He lives in Gray, Tennessee, with his wife and their daughter.